TIME OF DEATH

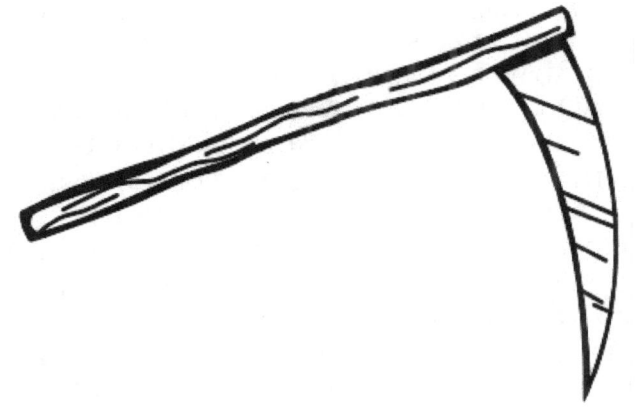

OTHER LIVING DEAD PRESS BOOKS

TIME OF DEATH

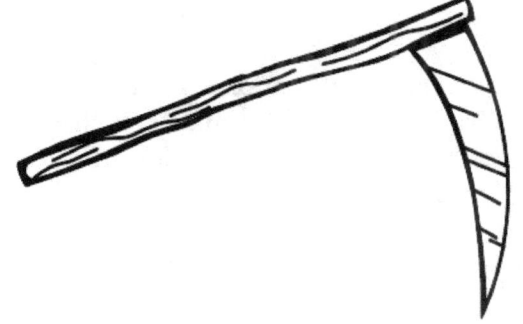

EDITED BY
ANTHONY GIANGREGORIO

TIME OF DEATH

Table of Contents

THE FATE TWIST

JOHN SABO

Kara Kramer had been looking forward to this night for quite some time. Inhumanly patient, she waited. All of her astrological charts pointed to this date. The 28th day of the 7th month of the 8th

year was her date with fate. Twenty-eight, minus seven, minus eight, equaled thirteen—her lucky number. Monday, the day of the week glorified by the moon itself, signified that the event would take place at night. The rune stones spelled out an end to the way that things had been, and an end to her lonely days. The tea leaves showed signs of a quest that was to be completed. Her palm laid out an intersection in her lifeline...again, a new beginning for her would start this night.

And the tarot, the tarot always revealed the dark stranger from her past coming back into her life. The tarot also showed the card of Death. She interpreted the ominous card as the death of her pitiful, lonely nights and the frustrating imaginary fantasies she concocted during her solo bedtime hours. As always, with death, there would be a new beginning. The birth of a new woman with purpose, who would wake next to a man of flesh and blood, who would love her beyond any of her previous dreams. Today was the beginning of a new world for her...only she had been waiting all day and nothing had shown itself.

Monday nights were always slow for her in this small town. She'd lived in a simple white house, next to the drive-in theatre, all her life. It was a simple life, but it was also a happy one. Kara was doing what she loved to do. Sure, she wished she had more money, more comfort and security. Who didn't? But at the end of the day, the bills were paid, the house was in good condition, and there was food in the refrigerator.

Summertime always brought *great* business. Without a good summer, Kara would find herself scraping through winter and spring, pinching every penny, and stretching every pot of stew just to get by. But summertime was her salvation. Friday and Saturday nights were her busiest. The local high school kids, and even several private schools in the surrounding counties, would flock to her mystic shop after the evening's double feature, for glimpses into their futures—so hopeful. Some would come for readings, some would come to hear other people's readings—too afraid that their possible embarrassing future would be spilled out for their friends to hear—and some would come to buy little charms, trinkets or books to begin their own path down the corridor of the fantastical and the unexplained.

Being the town psychic was the family business, or at least all the family she'd ever known. It was a few months after Kara's father was killed in the Vietnam War—he died two months before she was born—that her mother turned the home into a mystic parlor. And before Kara could read a word, her mother had taught her to see imagery in the Tarot cards.

The widowed 'spooky' mother and her only child, were first scorned by the predominately Roman Catholic community. Ms. Betty Belle eventually made a welcome and friendly name for herself, first by offering to do free readings at the church bazaar every summer, and also by selling her homemade jellies, jams and pies, which were also an absolute favorite of the Parish preacher, Father Haney. So after doing all that, the friendly, psychic, single mother couldn't be all bad, could she?

Kara allowed her mind to drift back to tender thoughts of her mother. How she'd taught Kara the ancient ways of a forgotten, more magical time. About the important lessons about life, respect, and love, and how to wait for that perfect gentleman to come into her life. But when Kara turned seventeen, those lessons stopped without warning, when her loving mother was taken from her by cancer. Kara felt that something was happening, that something was changing in her mother before she passed. But being a teenager in high school, Kara had many other problems on her mind. In their final moments together, Kara's mother explained that she would have much rather spent her final days living, than spending them preparing to die.

Kara never forgot that.

She wondered if her mother was looking over her now, watching from heaven with pride in her heart for her daughter on this special night. Sometimes, Kara could feel her mother's presence, but not tonight. Maybe it was all the excitement, the unknowing of it all. Well, the specifics of what would happen this night to make her life so much better.

So Kara waited.

And waited.

And waited.

All day long she'd waited excitedly for her event to unfold. But the time was now a quarter past ten at night. Her eventful day was quickly running out of time.

The only way she could express her feelings was that of great suspicion. Yes, it was suspicion that flooded the night. Suspicion, which started as a shadow of the unknown, now lurking and looming all around her. Suspicion, which was a ghost that could only be seen from the corner of the eye. Suspicion, that crack of light sneaking under a locked door, into the darkened room where she stared in wonder, eyes wide open in anticipation.

It was the third time she'd looked at the antique grandfather clock in as many minutes, when she exhaled deeply.

She was crestfallen.

Then suddenly there was an omen. There was a white neon flash from outside, and rain began to *drip-drip-drip*.

The time was almost at hand.

Something would soon be happening.

Someone was outside!

And that someone had been there for a while. Waiting. Pondering deep questions. Her connection with the stranger was intensifying. The suspicion quickly turned to excitement, with a hint or more of warning or danger. Why wouldn't they come in? She

searched deeper, thinking of what she had foreseen. It was someone not unfamiliar to her. Someone from her past. Curiosity was
buzzing all through her mind. But curiosity was what usually got
her into trouble. Should she chance a peek out of the front window
to let the stranger know she was aware of their presence? No, she
decided to play this cool, and wait for the cosmic event to play out
as it should.

The rain began to fall heavier outside. Kara stood in the middle
of the room with her eyes closed, trying to center herself, to open
herself to that which was about to happen. Then she had a flash of
a vision.

Pigs.

Pigs? Why pigs?

Pigs and pigtails…her pigtails, and Grandpap's farm on the
ridge.

Knuckles wrapped her front door three times hard and fast,
and the mystery man's name screamed and echoed in her mind,
shattering her eyes open wide.

Danny Flannigan was the one Fate had delivered to her on this
night of nights.

She quickly brushed her fingers through her hair, and tested
her breath by breathing into her palm. Never in a million lifetimes
would she have believed that the man that she had quivering,
lower lip biting, trembling night time fantasies about, would be
the one to knock on her door this night.

She began breathing heavily and fanning her face frantically
with both hands. "My-my-my-my-my," she muttered to herself as
she wondered what Danny Flannigan could possibly want with
her, and at this hour. Her mind quickly entertained a thought of
savage fantasy which forced a euphoric, wide-eyed smile to her
face. Then the knuckles struck the door a bit harder with more
desperation.

"Coming!" she called out, giggling inside at the dual meaning of the word. She exhaled, stood up straight, squeezed her breasts together—forcing her naturally large features up and out a bit—and smiled as she opened the door.

"You know, I was just about to close," she said coyly. "Danny?"

"Hey, Kara." Danny said softly while removing his well-worn John Deere Logo Cap. "I wasn't sure if you'd remember me or not."

"Danny Flannigan! Of course I remember you!" Kara was all rosy cheeks and miles of smiles. Probably for a moment or two too long actually. She blinked and waved the awkward pause off with her hand. "Where are my manners? Come in! Come in and get yourself out of that rain!"

Kara reached out to encourage him inside. As her hand made contact with his shoulder, a deep chill coursed through her soul. Her giddy smile wavered more than a bit. She tried to pass it off as nothing.

"Please, come into the parlor and sit for a spell." She guided him to the sitting room, where her clients would wait to be called into her private sanctum for their readings. Danny sat down on the purple plush love seat, and Kara took her place right next to him; a little too close for his comfort, so he scooted a bit to the left. Kara noticed how uncomfortable he was, and tried to calm him with a smile. "Now, what can I do for you, Danny?"

Kara, I've come to profess my undying love for you, and to take you in a manly fashion right here, right now, were the words that Kara heard in her mind.

"Hmm?" Kara shook away the fantasy. "What was that?"

"Uhm…" Danny squinted a bit while unconsciously raising an eyebrow as if to question whether Kara was all there or not. "What I said was, is that I've got a pretty big problem that needs immedi-

6

ate attention. Hell, I'm not even sure you're gonna be able to help me." His gaze dropped to the floor, then shifted to her heaving cleavage.

Kara smiled wider, nodding. "How can I help?"

"This may sound a little on the unimportant side, but my dog's run off, and she's about due to pop with a full litter. She isn't answering me when I call out to her, and I'm afraid she took shelter somewhere 'cause of the rain. Normally I wouldn't be so worried, but her last litter, well, they were all still born 'cause she wouldn't tear open the birthing sacks. I know this is a little stupid, but I was thinking, Kara, what with you being a psychic and all…that…"

"That maybe I could point you in the right direction?" Kara interrupted calming and smoothly.

"Yeah, I guess." Danny's eyes found their way back to her chest for a moment, then he stared at the floor.

"Give me your hand." Kara's voice was welcoming and warm.

"What?" he asked unexpectedly.

"Give me your hand," she said matter-of-factly as she reached over and took hold of his left hand. Kara then placed her left hand over, and her right hand under his. The instant she touched him, she wished she hadn't.

Darkness and chains.

Screams and pains.

Years and lives of torture.

Children…all children. Dozens of children all screaming.

Crying.

Begging for death.

Blood.

Kara pulled her hands away, seemingly burnt by the connection. Danny was on his feet a second later, standing before her with a very concerned look on his face.

Kara still had her eyes closed, but could feel the evil peer at her from behind his eyes. She had to think fast. "You…you said the dog is female?" She tried to feign a trance. "What is her name? I can't see her."

Danny was unsure of what to do, but he sensed she'd seen something she shouldn't have. But as he watched her, he began to reconsider. Maybe she hadn't seen anything after all. But he needed to be sure; he had to know what the psychic had seen. "Sam, her name is Sam," he said.

Kara knew then that it wasn't a female, or a dog. It was a little boy. Danny was looking for a little boy who'd managed to escape him. "Did you bring anything that belonged to Sam? A leash, or chew toy perhaps?" she asked.

Danny smiled. "I thought you might need something like that." He reached into his denim jacket pocket and produced a collar. "Here."

"Shouldn't this be on the dog?" Kara asked.

Danny hadn't thought of that. "Well, I took it off when her condition progressed—for her comfort." He was still holding the collar out in front of him awkwardly. Kara reached out with a bit of hesitation to take it from him. When she did, her hand brushed the back of his hand, and once more, horrible images and tiny faces filled with pain flooded her mind. A child squatting in blackness, his leg throbbing with pain: alone, cold, too scared to make a sound, too scared to open his eyes. But where was he? She tried to pull the vision back, and saw a barn, an old barn, blackened and grayed by weather and time. Pulling back further, she saw a house that seemed familiar from memory. Then she saw the red, well-water pump and handle, the paint now faded from time, and knew where the child was.

"I don't see a dog, but I do see a place. I see a covered bridge, and yes, it's the old Henderson place; the brown tool shed to the left of the fish pond." Kara opened her eyes only to see Danny trying to see through her.

"The Henderson place huh? There hasn't been anyone there for almost ten years or so. You sure?" He was still trying to read her.

"It's just a feeling; flashes mostly. It's not an exact science, but it's all I have for you." Kara tried to reassure him with a smile.

Danny shoved a twenty into her hand and turned to leave, without so much as a thank you.

"Danny?" Kara was crushed. How could the man she had lusted over for so long be such a monster?

He turned to face her.

"You'll let me know if you get the dog back in good health, now, won't you?"

"Sure," Danny smiled. "No problem. Thank you." He turned and walked away, and this time didn't stop. He was gone seconds later with the front door slamming behind him. No doubt heading out to the Henderson place in his van.

Kara allowed herself just a few minutes to process everything she had seen. What was she going to do now? How could she make everything right? She opened her eyes and found a new focus. Centered, she had but one purpose now — to find the child before Danny did.

She was frantic as she ran through her house, gathering items: car keys, flashlight, a weapon. She would need some kind of weapon. The only thing close, aside from a steak knife, was an antique sacrificial knife that was ruby-studded in the hilt. It had been her mother's and was just for show, but the blade was long enough to appear somewhat menacing if waved at someone.

She hurried to her car and was soon driving away from her home. She made the left to head in the same direction as Danny's van. She knew the old abandoned Henderson farm branched off of the same lane that Danny's parents' farm was on. She also knew

Danny's grandparents' farm was a bit further back on the same lane, and that was where the little boy had fled to. She hoped Danny had enough of a head start to begin his way down the Henderson road, so that she could slip by and go on unnoticed to his grandparents' place.

Kara made a right turn up Switch Willow Hill Road. The road was a twisting, turning, serpentine path that went up through the ridge overlooking the little town below. She'd driven this road ever since she was sixteen, and under most circumstances loved the twisting and turning of it. It was hypnotic and relaxing, and she knew every curve like her favorite melody. But now, preoccupied now with finding the child, she wasn't enjoying the quick lefts and rights as she normally would.

She was also oblivious to the van parked dark and idle on Cunningham Court, just out of sight from the main road.

Flannigan Lane was an old dirt road that cut its way back deep into the hills like a crooked tree with uncountable branches. At the beginning of the lane, there were a few scattered houses, all with a couple of acres of land—all hillside though. As the road went on, it branched off to other farm houses deeper into the woods with flatter, more manageable, land. Danny's farm was about another mile down the road, and his grandparents' place was about a half mile past that, the farm the last lot on the lane.

As she came to the intersection to where the Henderson farm was, Kara stopped to peer down the road in hopes of seeing lights from Danny's van. She prayed that he'd believed her deception, and was frantically searching the wrong area. She then continued her way down the main road. She drove past her Aunt and Uncle's old place, where she used to spend summer weekends tending to their cows. Then past Danny's pig farm, the one he'd inherited from his parents, where she used to play with the younger, innocent boy that she'd known from her childhood.

The darkness seemed to be thickening around her little Volkswagen Bug. The road was closing in tighter and tighter, and the trees were compressing their way closer to the already narrow road. The rain was coming down hard, and the wind was gusting, thunder and lightning cracking and flashing.

Kara had always been happy with summer thunderstorms, but tonight, she couldn't get the thought of her poor little VW Bug getting stuck in the mud flinging from her spinning bald tires. The inside of her windows were beginning to fog up, when the older Flannigan farmhouse materialized out of the shadows.

She pulled her car up as close to the barn as she could, then quickly got out, shocked at the pounding force and size of the raindrops. It felt like liquid jelly beans were crashing down upon her head from bottomless buckets in the sky. One droplet hit her hand so hard, she nearly dropped her flashlight.

The barn doors were chained closed, but the wood was old, warped and rotted. Kara was able to pry one of the doors open a bit on the bottom where she could wiggle her way under the brace and into the barn. She ignored the cold wetness as she was immediately soaked to the bone both top and bottom.

"Hello?" she called out to the blackness, which was cut by the single beam of her flashlight. "Are you in here?" She waited a few seconds for a response but heard nothing but rain hammering the barn roof.

"I'm here to help you—*oh!*" Kara jumped back and shook her head violently, her hands trying to brush away the spider web she'd walked into. After regaining her composure, she made her way to the back of the barn, where there were steps that led to a small fruit cellar; the door was locked.

How did the child get down there? A flash of memory to her vision from earlier, and she remembered a broken leg. He must have fallen through the floor! She scanned the barn with her flashlight, and sure enough found a hole in the floor where the child had fallen through.

Cautiously, she made her way to that spot, and scanned the lower floor area with her flashlight. "Hello? Are you down there?" she called out again, just as the beam of light found a bare leg which was quickly pulled back into the shadows.

Kara looked around for a ladder, but the barn was pretty much empty. No rope to be seen, but there were plenty of bails of hay.

"Sam? Is that your name?" she called down to the child draped in blackness. "Sam, the door to get you is locked, and I can't find a ladder. So, I'm going to drop some bails of hay down through the hole in the floor so I can climb down and get you out of there. Okay?"

No answer.

Kara tumbled three bails of hay, end over end, to drop them down through the hole, then decided to drop one more for good measure. She hopped down into the hole and the hay cushioned her fall. She would be able to stack the bails up to get her and the child out with no problem. She made her way to the little boy, and clapped her hand over her mouth to silence a gasp of terror upon fully seeing him. The child's skin was bone white, and his eyes were wide as could be. Trembling, he tried to back away as far to the corner as possible.

"It's okay… it's okay. I'm here now. Everything's going to be fine." She tried to smile and hold back the tears welling up in the corner of her eyes.

The child started gasping for air, as tears began streaming down his cheeks. Kara knelt down to comfort and warm him. The little boy could no longer hold back the screams of his tortured body and mind, and crying and wailing like a wounded animal, the boy let loose an unholy fury that was hard to witness.

A hellacious death dirge was let loose upon the stormy night.

Kara sat there rocking him, unsure if she had the strength herself to do what she knew she had to do. She ran her fingers through his hair, and tried to calm him with her hushes. The screams eventually silenced and turned to quivering sobs. "Shhh…" she said. "You're okay. Everything's gonna be fine."

The child was clinging desperately to her, as she cradled him in her lap. She looked down, smiling at him. "My name's Kara. I knew I'd find you! Now, everything's going to fine, you'll see."

The little boy looked up at her with tear filled eyes and tried to speak. "M…m…my n…n…name's S…Sam… S…Sam Loo…"

Before he could finish, Kara thrust her knife through the child's throat. She felt the blade hit the vertebrae in his neck, and slide to the left. Crudely, in a sawing motion, she sliced and tore through Sam's neck, nearly decapitating him. Flesh and muscle and veins and sinews popped and snapped and gave way to spurts of blood. Warm midnight red gushed all over Kara. The boy's screams and sobs quickly turned into a savage spasm of exiting life, one that was quickly followed by a sudden stillness, then a frighteningly final and violent death rattle, which startled Kara almost to a point beyond madness.

Kara wiped the warm, crimson stickiness from her face, allowing her finger to linger for a moment on her lips, where she dared a taste of the child's blood.

In silence, for many minutes, she sat waiting. Sure enough, the hollow rumble of Danny's van rolled up to the barn and stopped. There was a rattle of a chain, then the creek of the two old wooden barn doors. She traced the heavy footfalls on the floor above her head from the entrance to the barn, all the way to the back. There was another rattling of a chain, then the drop of a lock. Light peered down the old wooden steps to the cellar, as Danny made his way down. He shined his flashlight on the lifeless body of his missing Sam, sprawled on the floor in a pool of the boy's blood.

His hand began to shake and the light beam began to dance over the body. The light then found Kara's feet, then moved up her red-stained dress, over her blood-splashed chest, to the hellish smile on her face.

"WHAT...DID...YOU...DO?" Danny screamed.

"I did this for you—for us!" Kara said calmly, still smiling.

"What?" Danny slowly staggered over to the small corpse on the floor.

"I did this so you wouldn't have to. So that we could be together, and you would never have to do this again. I did this for you—for both of us!" Kara's smile was now fading.

"He was mine... MINE... MINE!" Danny raged, his fists were now clenched and his words were being forced out with as much spit as he could gather. He knelt down in front of the dead child's body, completely unsure of what to do next.

"Danny, Fate brought you to me tonight. Fate brought us together. I love you, Danny! I always have." Kara crawled over next to Danny and tried to caress his face, but he pulled away. "Didn't I do good? Didn't I do good for you, Danny?"

"He was mine," Danny began to sob. "Mine!"

"Now I'm yours, Danny, I'm all yours! We'll get past this! You'll never have to do anything like this again, and we'll be happy—the two of us together." She reached out for his chin and gently turned his face back towards hers. "Kiss me. Tell me you love me!"

Danny slowly leaned in closer to Kara, as if he was going to kiss her. Her lips were moistened and ready for this perfect connection, on this night of nights.

She closed her eyes.

But then he veered to the right, to whisper into her ear. "I could never love you," he hissed.

Her eyes bolted open, either from his haunting words, or the pain of the knife he stuck into her, to then twist inside her rib cage. Kara gasped and coughed. She felt her blood spilling out through her lips, over her chin and splashing down between her deeply heaving breasts.

Danny leaned back so she could see him fully.

"You stupid bitch! You're not even my type!"

And with that, Danny let loose with a fury of stabs to Kara's face and neck, breasts and womb.

Daylight broke before Danny stopped mutilating the psychic's body.

Damn her for taking the boy away from him, he thought.

Then, as easily as breathing, he gathered himself into a man of resolve. "Well, the pigs'll eat good today," he said to himself.

And there will always be other little children.

Fate always brought him new children.

RU488

CRAIG CAUDILL

-1-

"We need more stuff!" my wife would often say. Or she'd say, "The Stiddom's and the Macey's have got new dishwashers. Fred Sampson has a new boat." And boy did he ever get a new boat. Not only did he get a new boat but he got a mistress and a hot swanky pure bred Mastiff that he calls Zeus. Along with the stock tips from Wall Street, it seemed as if Fred Sampson was set for life. All he did one day was shoot his first born with a sawed-off shotgun. It happened right in front of our eyes. My wife and I were sitting on the front porch and Fred starting chasing little Doug out the front door but Doug wasn't fast enough to escape the blast.

Blaaaaaaaaaaaaaam! Glass sprayed with Doug's body flying out the door to land on the front lawn, twitching. He was gone.

Within minutes a mortician showed up with balloons, cameras, and sexy super models, congratulating them on their new lease on life. On the news, Fred said he felt sexier, younger and more virile then he had in years. Perhaps it was the mistress and the mutual breakup with his wife who last I heard was a lesbian working on a budding career in folk music. After forty years of marriage, shooting Doug was the break they needed to create their own lives.

As time went on, more and more children—mostly *firstborns* and children that parents wished they never had—were being systematically *offered* for the *Cause*. They would get on TV, showing off in their sexy cars or vacationing in the Cayman Island.

For others it was simply to have gay guys come to their house, redecorating with new furniture and changing lives altogether with the latest hair styles. With a new spare room, former fathers everywhere got that den they always wanted. Or former mothers got that room they always wanted for social gatherings or to display their dolls and other collectibles.

It all somehow looked easy and fun. On television there was a reality show where I saw parents feeding children to hungry bears with cameras attached to their heads, as they tore the children to ribbons. The other day, my local cable provider added a new package deal where you get a channel specifically about boa constrictors that swallow children and digest them for days. If you're lucky, you can catch this on both east and west coast channels so you never miss a thing.

As interesting as this may be, I still loved my son, and my wife did, too, but somehow she managed to turn all this off. Periodically, she would ignore him and even limited her displays of affection to three hugs a day, then to two, and eventually to just one to finally nothing at all. Without her, Chad only had his father to lean on, which my wife didn't approve of.

"What's the matter with you? People are beginning to look at us funny," she would say. "What kind of man are you? Everybody else is living the good life, and here we are living like a couple of classless losers; we should be having fun."

"Baby, we'll be fine. I'll ask my boss for a raise and everything will be fine," I would assure her.

"No, that's not what I'm talking about and you know it."

"Yes I know, but since it's not mandatory, I think Chad can stick around for a while. He's not hurting anyone, and I happen to love him."

"Oh, is that so?" She started screaming.

"Yes I do, he's actually quite a lot of fun."

"Look," she said, "I'm sure he's great, and I love him, too. I gave birth to him. But we have a crisis on our hands, can't you see that? We have wars and shortages of food. In some countries people are starving to death or gagging from the smell of another person's feces due to improper sanitation."

"Yeah, but we're not in Hawaii or the Netherlands. We have more options," I said soothingly

"But what about RU488?"

It began with Proposition RU486, which in many ways became the new September 11 mantra of the far-far right. After 2015, the population skyrocketed. A minor political cult emerged and came into power called the Children of Abraham. As the country grew weaker, they implemented Proposition 486 which limited marriage licenses to select groups and even the number of children. The population was so high by then that no one questioned it. Then came Proposition RU487, which sterilized everyone temporarily for ten years until things finally eased up.

Proposition RU488 was voted for unanimously in both the House and Senate. It was even backed by the Pope, and became effective in just three short days. Overnight, prison populations began to diminish, which freed tax burdens on American families.

In the beginning, I was a fan of 486, because it saved billions of our tax dollars. So when other people began to disappear like people who suffered from mental retardation or the disabled, I was okay with it. In a way like most people, I secretly wished for something like this to happen for a long time. But never in my life would I say such a thing out of fear of being looked upon as a bad person.

I never thought I'd see the day of this kind of feverish convenience on behalf of families. Some likened it to God telling Abraham to sacrifice Isaac but somehow God never sent an angel to put a stop to it. Instead there would be people running around with cameras, waiting for such visual opportunities for tabloid news programs and reality shows.

One day, I found my wife in Chad's room creating a pile of toys and clothes in the middle of the floor. As I watched in the doorway, I didn't have to ask to know that she was making room. I could see it in her eyes. *But why was she doing this?* I wondered sadly. Did we really need to keep up with the Joneses? I just wanted to grab her and shake as hard as I could, but that wouldn't stop her from throwing Chad out of her life. And where was Chad?

I began looking around the house, the living room, the hallway and it wasn't long before I found him hiding underneath the kitchen table.

"Hey, big guy, what are you doing under there?"

Chad said absolutely nothing which horrified me.

"Hey, Chad, is everything okay? Is this your new fort? Well, I had a kitchen table fort when I was your age, and your uncle Paul had one even more than I did. But it turned out he had a foot fetish. I blame his aunt Sandy for that one." Upon saying this, I realized that this may absolutely make no sense to a three-year-old.

"Mommy doesn't love me anymore."

"What? Why would you say something like that about Mommy?"

"Because she won't let me play with my toys," he said with great sorrow and uncertainty.

"You want your toys? Hold on, I'll get ya some toys."

I left him there because I didn't want him to see the tears in my eyes. Right now Chad was in a dark place and I had to somehow fix this, but by the time I got to my wife, I found myself face to face with five police officers standing in my living room. I remember a day when officers looked like officers, but now they dress like the SWAT team twenty-four hours a day, seven days a week.

"Can I help you, fellas?"

Then I was hit from behind and knocked unconscious.

-2-

Perhaps one of them did answer my question, I'll never know. All I remember is waking up on the floor of a small white room with absolutely nothing inside it. No bed, chair, toilet, window or even a door. Just stark white, except for when I reached out and saw my hand or I looked down at my feet. If anyone else had been there, I would never know it.

"Good morning, Mr. Morgan, we were beginning to think you wouldn't be joining us. I trust you slept well?"

"Who said that?" I looked around but there was no one. Just the whiteness.

"My name is Wade Sunshine, believe it or not. It may sound silly considering I fancy myself a serious person. My great-great grandparents were fourth generation Hippies and they legally changed their names a long time ago, so I have this snazzy last name that somehow makes people smile. What do you think? Does it make me sound snazzy?"

"Where are you?"

"Somewhere safe I suppose."

"Okay, so where am I?"

"You're in the safest place in the world; no one can touch you here. It's like playing a video game. You die and you get to start over again, only this time with options."

"I don't understand, what do you mean by *options*?"

A section of wall the size of a door on my left began to lift up, and I found myself looking at two men behind Plexiglas. Instead of being dark and sinister looking, they looked calm and properly groomed in the most wholesome way. Manicured hands, trimmed moustaches, and perfectly tan. They looked well-fed too.

"We all have options, you know that Mr. Morgan, and we at the Networks would like to help you know what they are," the man on the right said. It was Wade Sunshine.

"I just want to get out of here," I said

"Well, so do we. We're all adults here after all. We have better things to do than just sit around and talk about issues. You need to know that ultimately we're on your side," Wade Sunshine said.

"That's very kind of you, but I'd appreciate it if you'd stop calling me Mr. Morgan."

"Oh I'm so sorry about that. Here, let's see what I can find." He was patronizing me, I could tell. He looked down at a file in his hands, turning some of the pages. "Let's see here, Tom Morgan, Cameron Corgon, ah, here we go. Tom Morgan. Yes, well that's your name, Mr. Morgan, so that's what we'll be calling you. Wouldn't you agree, Stanley?"

Wade looked at the other man, Stanley, who in turn just slightly nodded in agreement without saying anything. Seeing the two of them interact this way, I somehow felt trapped inside absolute absurdity. There was nothing I could do about this. I was either going to do everything their way or I was going to die, as everything was going to be eventually done their way if they wanted it. Then the smiles were gone except in the eyes. Which said to me that things were about to get more serious. Stanley leaned in and addressed me. "Mr. Morgan, we don't like unpleasant things. We know you want to get back home to your lovely wife. Especially after all she'd been through these past six months."

"Where is she?"

"She's at home safe and sound, and don't worry, we have a guard on protective duty with her right now as we speak. No one can hurt her."

"Harm my wife? I wouldn't do anything to hurt her. I love her. She means everything to me." Which was true.

"Really?" Wade Sunshine asked. "Then why does she go without? Why must she exist day after day, not dressed in the finest clothes that all her friends are wearing? Why isn't she driving a luxury car? Her friends don't even talk to her now because she's doesn't fit into the club anymore."

"Are you kidding me?" I asked.

"No I'm afraid not, and if you had paid attention, you could see that. I mean, come on, Mr. Morgan, wake up! You need to take a good look at yourself. How are things at work? When was the last time you were promoted?"

"What!" I said.

"Be honest now, when was the last time you've ever been promoted for anything?" Stanley asked.

"I don't know. Two years ago maybe."

"Did you hear that, Wade?" Stanley asked, leaning towards Wade's direction.

"What?" Wade said, pretending to be focused on something else.

"He said two years. It's been two years since he's got a big promotion. I bet the big boss is happy to not have to promote such a loser as our friend Mr. Morgan."

"Pathetic," Wade Sunshine said with a shake of his head.

"Yes, I agree, pathetic and selfish!" Stanley said.

"Any man who can barely take care of his family shouldn't even be allowed to have one unless he's prepared to make a sort of sacrifice," Wade said. "Any man who can't carry his weight anymore is not worthy of the riches others proudly take for granted. The most he could hope for is cremation."

"Now wait a minute!" I said but Wade continued.

"It's the least you could do considering how much your wife suffers so," he said. "She worries herself sick, wondering when you'll come around." Wade was looking his most sincere.

"I'm not doing this. My wife can wait for ever for the things she wants. He's my son and I won't do it." I said, knowing I had a snowball's chance in Hell of convincing them.

Wade went through the file and held up the standard release form every parent or planning-to-be-parent signed sometime before they got married.

"You signed this, and don't act like you don't know what this is. Everyone signs this on the day of their marriage." Wade walked right up to the Plexiglas and plastered the release form on the window.

"I know what it is. But guess what? Chad isn't our first born," I said. "Our first born died during child birth. Chad's the one who lived. So technically we made our offering." I hoped something I said would get through to them.

"No, no, no, it doesn't work that way!" Stanley shouted.

"Did he actually say that? Oh my God, I can't believe he said that. Is everything a loop hole to you?" Wade asked.

"No, I didn't say that. What I meant was..."

"Do I need to remind you that two years ago our beloved President, who is fighting for the cause of eradicating population overgrowth, gave up his only begotten son?" Stanley asked.

"Yes, how brave and heroic he was. He could have easily opted out by playing the Presidential card and said no, just like our cowardly friend Mr. Morgan. But he picked himself up from the ashes like the phoenix he truly is and gunned down his very own son right there in the halls of the White House," the patriotic Wade said.

"And do you know how the people rewarded him for this act of bravery?" Stanley inquired.

"Four terms, and that being the President is once again considered *sexy*. And we're on our way again; we even got Hawaii back from Sweden. Sweden!" Wade emphasized the seriousness of Sweden, like it was the big sleeping giant after the rise and fall of China. But anyone knew that one of China's problems was quality control.

Eventually no one could afford anything, because all the best jobs were outsourced. With the increase of cutthroat salaries, markets crashed and that's when Sweden stepped in.

"Yes, Sweden," Stanley spat back in agreement. His eyes were cold and piercing, as if he were focusing on my face, trying to set it on fire with heat ray vision. If I'd been lucky, they would have spared me the world history lesson. But sadly I was once again given the sleeping giant lectures. From Mexico to Guam, to the supposed Tesla Death Ray built in Cambodia which was believed to be pointed straight at the United States. I wasn't spared the rhetoric. It was never-ending because they had a point to make. Eventually it came to me and my responsibilities to my country, my community, and the wife that I've publicly shamed by not fulfilling the promise I'd made.

"So, what is it you want, hmmm?" Wade asked. "Is it a new car? An island in the Caribbean? There's still quite a few left. I could check into this if you like."

"No, I don't want an island. I don't want anything. I just want to go home. I've done nothing wrong," I said.

"Oh, I guess we're mistaken then." Wade looked at Stanley, then around the stark room in comedic confusion. "We feel you've neglected your patriotic duties. We feel that you're compromising the quality of life here on Earth and it would be so much better if you'd just do your part." Wade's voice was soothing and assuring.

Stanley stepped closer, looking at me carefully and biting his lower lip to give the allusion that we were making a bargain. "We're prepared to pay you handsomely for this dilemma. Mark my words. We understand your plight but there are others who will suffer far more because of what you cling to. He may be a son to you, but he's also a gift you can give to others and to yourself. Why deprive yourself of resources or upgrades of social standing by clinging to the old ways?" Stanley pleaded.

"I can't do it. It's not natural."

"You can and you will because you know it's right, because of RU488 we're a stronger nation," Wade said proudly. "Crime is down, overpopulation is finally coming down. Diseases are all but eradicated now thanks to RU488 and people are living longer lives. We couldn't have asked for a better plan. We're finally catching up. America is strong again."

"I agree. We are stronger because of RU488, and as far I'm concerned the Swedes can have their Space Race; we've been there already," Stanley said. "It's harsh out there. We don't need to be there when it's old news."

"I can't do it, he's my son and I love him. He means everything to me. I only want my son. I don't want anything else in this world. Please don't make me do this." I begged Stanley but his eyes seemed to be begging me for sanity, to come to my senses.

"Look at it this way," Wade reasoned. "He'll always be a part of you. He'll always be inside your heart. Nothing will ever take that away from you."

"No, I can't, and there's nothing you can say to change my mind. Don't you get it? There's nothing you can say that can make me change my mind. There's nothing at all."

Wade smiled, but when I saw his cold eyes, I realized that I was terrified, despite my resolve.

"Oh, Mr. Morgan, we'll see about that."

-3-

Though I never thought I would agree, they finally wore me down after days of no food and water, and we negotiated an iron clad deal which would be promising for them, because what I was supposed to do would be aired on television to mark a supposed anniversary of when God spoke to Abraham. I was to take Chad to the mountains build a makeshift altar. Then kill him with a knife and throw him upon the fire. Wade said it was going to be live on the network that very night, and if I wanted to, like many before me, I could have my very own talk show, and I could interview celebrities and poke fun at dignitaries from around the globe.

After I signed the contract, and was fully aware of the consequences if I defaulted, I was returned to my home.

After eating I had gone right to bed, not even bothering to shower, and when I woke up I could barely remember anything that had happened. I found myself lying in bed with my wife snoring next to me. Perhaps I sounded just as bad, but for some reason it sounded perverse coming from her. She sounded like a chimpanzee drooling all over herself and the bed. The sudden urge to beat her over the head with a hammer or choke the life out of her was so overwhelming that it took all of my willpower not to act on it. In that instant I realized I didn't love her anymore.

I don't know when I fell out of love with her but it must have happened some time ago. Sometimes we're followers to the great scheme of things because we don't know any better. I realized my individuality was lost long before I ever gave it up. They, whoever 'they' are, more then likely had decided my fate long before I was even born. Perhaps anything I ever wanted in this world was pretty much shaped and formed by the options only given to me like a pointed question, with likely predictable and expected outcomes.

-4-

It was early in the morning as I drove Chad to the Pavilion, a park known for its open fields and hilly mountainous appeal. In the sky, I could see new helicopters hovering about here and there as they tried to get a good shot.

After building the altar I set it on fire, as Chad was sleeping in the car. The knife in question was in my right hand coat pocket. I was going to take him out of the car and lay down next to the altar, then stab him and triumphantly throw him onto the fire and live out the rest of my cowardly life without a real son and perhaps adopt a child that looked nothing like me, raising him as if he were my very own. But if I did go through with this, more than likely I wouldn't be able to live with myself. I just couldn't do it to Chad.

As I laid my son next to the altar, the wind became stronger, creating unpredictable dramatic patterns within the flames. For the viewers at home it would have been entertaining no doubt.

With Chad still sleeping, somehow it was easier to raise the blade above my head. I was going to take this opportunity to stab quickly and get it over with finally and I was about to do it, God help me when Chad's eyes opened and he looked around, then finally up at me, our gazes locking. He didn't even look at the blade, although I'm sure he could see it. Instead, he smiled innocently in his sleepy nonjudgmental way that only knows love.

"Good morning, Daddy," he said, before falling back to sleep again, wrapped up and warm in his blanket. That's when I hesitated. I must have held the knife there for two full minutes before I felt the presence of a cameraman standing behind me.

"Go on, Mr. Morgan, you can do it," the man whispered.

"Huh?" I turned and there he was with his camera.

"I said, you can do it."

Perhaps it was pure sickness that overwhelmed me at the thought of someone cheering for me to kill my son. I then looked at Chad and lowered the knife, because I just couldn't do it.

"Wait, Mr. Morgan, if you want, we can go to commercial. I'll give you a gun. I think that might make it easier on you. What do you think?" he asked, trying to be sincerely helpful.

What did I think as my knife went straight into his chest? I thought that murdering people was much easier than I thought it would be. I stabbed the cameraman two more times before picking up the gun after it fell out of the back of his pants. I grabbed Chad and clumsily got into my car, bumping my head as I leaned in to put him in the backseat. Then I drove off, the helicopters still hovering overhead. I made a mad dash across town, trying to think where would be the safest place to hide. Perhaps I could join an underground movement. But as far as I knew, there wasn't any group of wandering nomadic rejects creating their own society. In a dream world it's always convenient, but reality it is not.

There was nowhere for me to go, and after an hour of hiding in a grocery store parking lot, I decided I had to face my fate and go home. Whatever fate had in store for me, so be it.

When I arrived home, the place was completely empty. No police, no Network TV executives, nor my wife. For just a brief moment it was just Chad and me alone, to what would be the last calm moment together as father and son. Everything seemed somehow emptier than before, like it never really was my house in the first place. It felt generic, even as I took him up to his bedroom.

The feeling was so overwhelming. I barricaded the door with the dresser, hoping somehow that this would protect us. Moments later, I heard footsteps and my wife screaming about something downstairs as she entered the house. I didn't have to know word for word to understand what she was talking about. The police had also arrived, and judging from the footsteps and voices, it sounded liked there were four or five.

How did I rationalize my actions? I would have to say I was saving Chad from them. I was saving Chad from having his murder witnessed by complete strangers, and somehow this helped me. I was saving Chad from the degradation. So before they broke down the door and pushed away the dresser, I laid the pillow over my son's face and pressed as hard as I could. When he began to struggle, I didn't have the heart to go through with the whole thing of smothering him, so I removed one hand from the pillow, took the gun from my waistband, and shot him two times. Although it wasn't easy, the relief was instant, and in time I was glad I did it. Because true time does heal all wounds, as they say in the Bible and television almost everyday.

After Chad was dead, I knew there would be balloons and streamers, women in bathing suits with large breasts, which makes absolutely no sense to a foot man like my brother.

By the time the door was forced in, I was sitting on the floor in the corner of the room, crying.

-5-

Within three days I got my rewards for offering my son to the RU488 cause. The second prize was a cruise ship package, which I took as the opportunity I needed to disappear and leave my wife forever. From there I boarded a commercial import ship leaving Cuba going straight for England.

Even though I felt like they were going to turn around and take me back to that white room for what I'd done to the cameraman, they didn't. I was really free. For three months I stayed in London before I finally journeyed to Sweden, and when I finally arrived there I felt they understood me.

Perhaps they knew what I had gone through and what I had to do to survive. Brainwashing was never brought up but I'm sure this was part of my dark past that I had awakened from. I'll never understand fully on how they felt about me, but I felt completely accepted and nurtured there. I was a functioning human being again, relearning everything they could possibly teach about life and love.

I met a woman six months ago. Her name is Martha, and we married two months ago.

I bought us a small cottage on a hillside and I spend hours just sitting there and staring out at the beauty of nature.

I try not to think of my lost son too much, for if I did, I know that wall I have built to block off those terrible memories will come crashing through, and I don't think I would be able to return from that if it ever happened.

Did I tell you that Martha is pregnant? She's four months along, which is one of the reasons I married her so fast after meeting her.

I want our child to grow up with parents that are married.

It's a boy by the way.

I already have a name picked out and Martha says it's fine.

We're going to call him Chad.

DEATH.COM

ANTHONY GIANGREGORIO

"We need some more beers over here!" someone yelled, the 2012 New Year's Eve party in full swing.

"I'll get them, Susan," Ray said.

"Would you be a dear and do that, Ray? Thank you so much." Susan Willows (formerly Susan Carpenter) smiled so that her ridiculously-white teeth seemed to glow in her mouth. The day they invented teeth-whitening gels, Susan had been the first one in line, eager to buy a thousand tubes. Not that Ray Garrison minded. Now in his forties, he'd had a crush on Susan since high school.

Susan looked great for her age, too, her figure the same size it was back in high school. Unfortunately she was married now; Ray's dreams crushed that day ten years ago when Susan had married another of their high school classmates, Brad Willows.

He'd never liked Brad back then, though over the years the man had grown on Ray. Brad had been captain of the football team, valedictorian, the guy who had it all, including Susan, who was homecoming queen her senior year. The two had been prom king and queen also, and Ray had no choice but to grin and bear it.

Ray's failed marriage was a thing of the past and it had been destined to fail from the start. He'd never gotten over Susan, the high school crush that had lasted his entire life.

The party was at Susan and Brad's house, a get-together that happened once a year ever since after their five year high school reunion.

Ray left the living room where everyone was partying and entered the kitchen through the swinging white door. Upon stepping inside, he saw two more people from high school in the corner, though they were a little busy to notice him.

Rick Masters and Mary Higgins were making out. Mary was sitting on the counter, her legs wrapped around Rick's bare ass, which Ray could see easily as the man's pants were down by his ankles. He was thrusting into Mary like he was a living piston, and Ray could see Mary's eyes were rolled up into the back of her head, her mouth opening and closing with each thrust inside her.

"Don't mind me, guys, just getting some more beers," Ray said with a grin. He went to the refrigerator, grabbed a six pack, and exited without saying anything else.

The screwing couple never so much as glanced his way.

Pushing the kitchen door with his elbow, Ray left the couple to their own devices. When he entered the living room again, the noise hit him like a wave. The music was on far too loud and everyone was yelling to be heard over it. The party was a great success, with only a few people not showing up. A couple of people had had previous engagements and one of their regulars had died recently, which had come to a shock to them all. Before the party had gotten going, they'd all gathered into a circle and spoken a few words about their lost friend, who hadn't had a wake or funeral.

"Here's Ray with the beers. It's about fucking time, asshole," Bob Richardson barked, the rest of the group laughing.

"He was probably jerking off in the toilet again," Marco Balducci roared, causing the rest to laugh along.

"Ha, ha, Marco you're so goddamn funny I can't stop myself from laughing," Ray said, feeling like an idiot the instant he replied with the clichéd comeback. He placed the six-pack on the table and hands dove in, the beers disappearing in an instant, leaving behind the cardboard six-pack holder.

Ray took a step back, taking in the people he once called 'friends.' As he looked at each face, he hated to admit it but he really didn't know them anymore—except for Susan that is, who he talked to frequently on the phone.

Once a year on New Year's Eve, gathering at Susan's house, did not make life-long friends, it made acquaintances. Marco said something and everyone laughed, then they clinked beer bottles and drank.

The next two hours went by in a blur for Ray, the time filled with drinking, talking and laughter. Midnight came and went and everyone yelled, *"Happy New Year!"* when the clock hit midnight.

Finally, around three in the morning, the party slowed and everyone was gathered on the couch and surrounding chairs, talking softly. The music was off and the television was on, a re-run of *The Bachelor* playing now that the festivities were over on TV; no one was watching it.

Ray was sitting off to the side in an easy chair, sipping a beer, and he tried not to let his gaze fall on Susan and Brad, who were sitting together on the left side of the couch. Rick and Mary were on the right side of the couch and were talking quietly together. Ray had found out a little while ago that their little 'hook-up' in the kitchen meant nothing to either of them and was only for fun. Apparently, every now and then when the two were between relationships, they would get together and screw like bunnies. *Fuck buddies* was the proper term.

Marco and Bob were standing behind the couch, talking about some chick Marco was trying to bang.

"You okay over there, Ray?" Susan asked.

Ray looked over from Bob and Marco to see Susan was looking right at him.

"Huh? Oh yeah, doin' great," he said, forcing a smile.

"So, Ray," Bob began. "Seeing anyone right now?"

"No, haven't found anyone, thanks for asking," he replied.

"You should go on one of those couple's dating sites," Rick suggested. His left hand—the one closest to Mary—was mysteriously hidden from view thanks to Mary sitting on it. She was squirming in her seat and Ray had an idea what that hand was doing.

Ray shook his head. "Those sites aren't for me."

"I heard there are a lot of desperate chicks on those sites," Marco added, getting in on the conversation. "I hear the divorced ones are the most desperate. Buy 'em dinner and tell 'em they're pretty for their age and you'll be gettin' blown in the backseat of your car before the date's half over."

Susan turned her head so she was looking up at Marco standing right behind her. "Wow, such class you have, I can't imagine why you're still single."

Marco barked out laughter, then took his hand and brought it up and down over his body. "I have to stay single, Susan, wouldn't want to take *all this* off the market. Too many women out there still need my lovin'. "

Susan let out a bark of laughter herself and Mary tittered a little, thanks to Rick's hand doing its job.

"Oh please, you're Italian stallion routine is as old as *Saturday Night Fever*," Susan rebutted.

Marco shrugged his shoulders in a *you have a right to your opinion* gesture. "Maybe so but it works on more women than you might think."

"I gotta use the can," Bob announced and went to the bathroom. Everyone chatted while he was gone and a few minutes later he returned. He was holding his Blackberry in his hand now, after having surfed the internet while in the bathroom. He went to Brad and patted him on the shoulder. "Hey, Brad, a buddy sent me a link to a new website that I think everyone will find pretty interesting. You got your laptop handy? This screen is too damn small to see anything."

"Sure, give me a second," Brad said and got up, crossed the room and picked up his laptop from an end table in the corner. He opened it and waited for it to boot up, then sat next to Susan again.

On the TV, a bleach-blonde had been turned down and hadn't gotten a rose. She was in a limousine as it drove away, crying, as if the love of her life had ditched her and her life would never be the same, that she would never be able to love again for the rest of her life. Such bullshit.

The chime on the laptop sounded, letting Brad know the machine was all set and he repositioned it on his lap so he could type. "Okay, Bob, what's the site?"

"Death.com," he said simply.

Brad turned to look at Bob. "Death.com? What is it, some sort of horror site?"

"No, not really. Just type it in; it's easier to just show you than try to explain it."

Brad googled the site but it didn't come up on a simple search. "Not here," Brad said.

Bob was standing behind Brad, leaning on the back of the couch. He pointed at the page on the screen. "Scroll down, I know what to look for."

Brad began scrolling down the pages, then went to the next one, then the next page. Finally, on page three, Bob said, "There, that's it."

Brad moved the cursor so that it was hovering over the site Bob pointed to. Next to the name was a skull and cross bones. Brad clicked on it and the screen went black.

Susan let out a sigh as she sat next to Brad, watching the screen go dark, then it became bright and the site came up. The skull and crossbones dominated the screen and below it were three white rectangles for typing in information.

"Wow, impressive," Brad said sarcastically as he looked at the screen.

"Shut up," Bob snapped. "Here hand me the laptop."

Brad did as requested and Bob balanced it on the back of the couch so he could type. He tapped a few keys and handed the computer back to Brad, who looked at the screen and saw that there were numbers in the three boxes. From the second he looked at them he was pretty sure he knew what the numbers were by the way they'd been entered: 225-66-7891. A social security number.

"Is that what I think it is?" Brad asked.

"Yeah, that's my social. Go 'head and hit enter."

By now the others, curious, had moved around either to the side of Brad or next to Bob so they could see the screen. On the television, *The Bachelor* ended and the next reality piece of shit came on.

Brad hit enter and the screen flashed to what looked like a slot machine, such as one found in a gambling casino, only it wasn't fruit that was spinning in the window, it was numbers.

A few seconds went by before the numbers began to slow and finally they stopped on 3/12/2013.

"Oh shit, that ain't good," Bob said with a chuckle.

"What's not good? What does it mean?" Susan asked, now staring at the screen as if she was afraid to take her eyes away.

"Well," Bob said, "according to this date, I have three months and change before my time of death." He pointed at the screen. See, this site tells you when you're gonna die. All you do is type in your social security number and your date comes up."

"What?" Marco asked, guffawing. "Sounds like a load of horseshit."

Bob turned to him. "Oh really? Then go 'head and put yours in and see what comes up. I dare you."

Marco hesitated for a few seconds, but Ray could see that he was going to give in, if only because he was being dared. Ray thought back to when they were in high school and had a deja vu feeling. They were middle-aged adults and something as silly as a dare should not have made Marco want to do something he didn't want to, but sometimes the child inside everyone never really leaves.

"Fine," Marco said. "Brad, give me that computer so I can type in my social."

"Here."

Marco took the laptop, placed it on the back of the couch, and typed in his social, then hit enter before handing it back to Brad. When Brad placed it on his lap again, the slot machine window was working as the numbers rolled at a blurring speed and began to slow.

Finally, the numbers 7/2/13 came up.

"Well, Marco," Bob ribbed. "According to this, you get to the middle of next year to get your shit in order." He laughed. "But hey, you got longer than me. Hell, I'll be dead by St. Patrick's Day!"

"Do me next, I want to try," Mary said from the left of Brad. He was going to hand her the laptop when she said, "No, I'll tell you my social. I'm not worried about any of you guys. Hell, if you want my identity you can have it." She rambled off nine numbers and Brad put them into the boxes and pressed 'enter.'

The slot window appeared and a minute later the date of Mary's death was there.

12/31/13

"New Year's Eve?" Mary said. "This thing says I'm going to die on New Year's Eve next year?"

"Maybe you better skip the party scene next year, Mary," Bob suggested with a laugh. But he saw she looked scared and he patted her arm. "Hey, lighten up, it's all in fun, it's not real."

"Neither is a Ouija board, Bob, but I don't fuck around with those," Mary replied.

"Relax, Mary, it's not a real site, it's all pretend," Rick said. "Here, I'll do mine next. Give it here, Brad."

Brad handed Rick the laptop, Rick typed in his social and a few seconds later, they were all staring at the numbers in the slot window.

"Shit, 12/31/13," Bob said. "That's the same date as Mary." He looked Rick in the eyes. "Maybe you guys kill each other in a jealous rage or something. Murder suicide!" He was laughing now, loving the discomfort in Rick's eyes.

"Ha, ha, asshole," Rick said. "Keep it up and you're gonna get a bloody nose for your trouble."

"Yeah," Mary agreed. "I don't think it's funny either."

"Oh, relax, you two. I'm just playing with ya. It's all in good fun." Rick pointed to Brad and Susan. "Why don't you guys go next so Mary and Rick will feel better."

Brad looked at Susan, his eyes asking permission.

Susan only shrugged. "Go 'head, babe. It's not like it's real."

Brad punched in his social security number and then pressed 'enter.' A few seconds later, he was reading the date on the screen. "9/15/16. Huh, well at least I have a few years left," he joked and turned to Susan while he handed her the laptop. "Here, Suz, punch in yours next."

She took the computer and did as she was told, and a few seconds later the date came up.

"8/23/18," she read aloud. "About two years after Brad's death. I wonder why that is?"

Before anyone could reply, Bob grabbed Ray and pushed him close to Susan. "Here, let Ray try. He hasn't gotten a turn yet."

"Do you want me to type it in for you, Ray?" Susan asked.

"No, I think I'll pass this time. This isn't a game I like. It's so…morbid."

"Oh come on, Ray," Bob cajoled. "Don't be a pussy all your life. We all did it and now you have to, too."

"Yeah," Mary agreed. "If I'm gonna die at this time next year, the least you could do is find out when it's your time."

"Here, here," Rick added. "We did it, now it's your turn. Don't wimp out on us now."

"They have a point, Ray. We all did it and you're the only one left," Brad added.

Ray, not wanting to be disliked and have everyone berate him, finally held his hands up to stop them from talking. "Okay, okay, you win, I'll do it. Susan, give me the laptop, I'll punch my own social in if you don't mind."

She handed him the computer, and as she did, she had to lean forward. Ray took the laptop and got a wonderful view of her cleavage. His eyes locked onto it and it took all of his willpower to pull his gaze away. He didn't want anyone to see him looking, especially Brad and even worse, Susan.

Placing the laptop on the side of the couch, he typed in his so-cial, but changed the last number to a six when it should have been a seven. After all, if it was all in fun then a number was a number. When he hit 'enter,' the window began to spin and then a big red error sign appeared on the screen, flashing like an alarm.

Bob, standing behind him patted his arm. "Try again, Ray," he said. "You must have hit a wrong number." He leaned in close to Ray's ear. "My buddy told me you can't lie, it knows if you aren't entering your real social."

Ray felt like he'd been caught cheating on a test when he was back in high school, but he put a smile on his face and nodded. "Oh, uh, yeah, I must have hit a wrong key." He didn't give it much thought as to how the hell the site could know he was lying. He quickly retyped his social, this time using the proper one. When he hit 'enter' the slot window appeared and the numbers began to spin. He didn't know why but his mouth was suddenly dry and there was a tightness in his chest. Why was he scared? It wasn't like it was real or anything.

The numbers stopped spinning and Ray read the date aloud: "4/21/21"

"Ha," Bob yelled. "Looks like Ray's gonna be the last of us above ground."

Ray stared at the numbers, feeling like he was going to faint. He thought to himself that if this was true, then he was looking at the day he would die.

Susan and Brad were having a discussion about just that, and soon Mary and Rick were joining in, both trying to guess why they had the same time of death.

Marco was doing the stereotypical Italian thing, trying to yell over everyone else to be heard as he talked to Bob, who was also talking.

The room was soon very loud, everyone discussing what they thought the dates could mean, and if they were true, what that bode for them all.

But it was all in fun and soon the conversation turned to other things, and Ray, who had been silent for most of the discussions, was soon pulled back into concepts of how long roofing shingles really last and if a snow blower was really needed even though they lived in New England. (In the old days everyone had to shovel.)

Brad had gotten up at one time and crossed the room to put the laptop down, but before he closed it, he typed in everyone's expiration date (it had been saved on the side of the screen) and printed it out, then handed each of them a copy.

"For reference," he joked. "One day we can check these and see if it was legit or not."

"Well, I for one sure as shit hope it's not. I'm the first to go!" Bob was laughing by the time he finished talking, thinking it all so much fun. "You assholes better give me a good send-off too. No crying and shit. I want a jazz band and everything."

Marco laughed so hard he was spitting. "Screw that! A pine box and a hole in the ground, that's what you deserve." The others laughed at this, especially when Bob started pouting.

Susan got up and walked over to Bob, rubbing his shoulder like a mother to a son. "Oh, Bob, now don't pout. You know Marco's kidding. We'll give you such a send-off people will think the President of the United States is getting buried."

Bob crossed his arms and smiled. "There, now that's more like it."

Once more the topic changed to other things and by the end of the party, the Death.com part of the night was all but forgotten and it was time for everyone to leave. Cheeks were kissed and hugs were given and promises were made to get together before next year's party.

Ray hugged Susan, holding her for just an extra second as he breathed in the smell of her hair. He finally let go, though he didn't want to.

Months passed uneventfully for Ray. He chatted with Mary and Rick by e-mail and Facebook a few times, and once Brad called him to ask his advice about installing hardwood flooring. (Ray had put in all new floors in his home a year earlier.)

Then one night, a few minutes after he'd gotten home from work, Ray received a phone call from Susan that woke him up to his own mortality.

"Hello?" he'd said upon answering his cell phone, assuming it was going to be a call just like a thousand other phone calls he'd had over his lifetime.

"Ray? It's Susan."

His heart skipped a beat at the sound of her voice. "Susan? Oh wow, it's so great to hear from you. How's Brad doing putting in those hardwood floors?"

"Fine, he did fine," she said, brushing the question off. "Ray, I…have some bad news to tell you." Her voice cracked and he heard her stifle a sob.

His mind raced with what could be so bad that it had her so emotional. When he'd asked about Brad, she hadn't acted like something had happened to her husband, so what could it be? He waited for her to speak.

"It's…it's Bob," she began, and he could hear her facade cracking as she began to cry. "He's…he's dead."

"What? How? Holy shit, I don't believe it."

"They say it was his heart. It hit him fast, the heart attack, I mean. It happened a few days ago at work, at the office. He was dead before the paramedics arrived. Oh, Ray, I can't believe it but he's gone."

"Jesus, we just saw him a few months ago at your New Year's Eve party," he said. "He seemed fine then. Healthy I mean."

"His sister called me. She was going through his address book and she saw my name and recognized it from when we were all in school together. She thought to call me. The wake is tomorrow night if you want to go. I can e-mail you the address if you like."

"Of course, send it to me."

"Okay, listen, I have to go, I still need to call Marco, Rick and Mary."

"Oh uh sure, of course."

"Okay, bye, I'll see you tomorrow night." She hung up.

Ray put the phone down and stared at a framed photo on the wall of him, Bob, Rick and the others. The picture had been taken at graduation and they were wearing their gowns, though their hats were long gone after being tossed into the air. They were all smiling, their future unwritten, a world of possibilities before them.

But that was all in the past now.

Though Ray was floored that Bob was dead, deep down he had to admit he was looking forward to the wake, even if it was for an excuse to see Susan again.

Over the next day he talked to Marco and Rick on the phone and then it was the night of the wake.

Upon walking into the funeral home, he immediately heard Marco's loud voice. Following it, he came to the room hosting Bob's wake. The casket was a closed one and he was glad for it. There had always been something creepy about staring at people when they were made up for the funeral services. They seemed so…fake, was the word that came to mind.

Some people said that the dead looked as if they were only sleeping, but Ray had always believed that was crap. They looked dead, simple as that, and the idea of death freaked him out to no end.

Entering the room, he saw the same thing he always did when he went to a wake. A few rows of chairs, about five deep, sometimes more, and in the front, the casket and the flower bouquets loved ones and friends had sent. As he moved through the half-full room of mourners, he stopped when he was right behind Marco, who was talking to Susan, Brad, Rick and Mary.

He didn't wait for Marco to stop talking to announce himself. If he did that, he would never get a word in. Marco was a typical animated Italian, full of life and loved to talk. Luckily, he wasn't a boring person and he was fun to listen to…as long as Ray wasn't too tired or had had a frustrating day. Then Marco could be downright grating on the nerves, but then…so would anyone else when Ray was in that kind of mood.

"Hey, guys, how's it going?" Ray said to Marco's back, the man promptly turned around, a smile coming to his face when he saw it was Ray.

"My man, Ray, it's good to see you," Marco said and shook Ray's hand.

"Yeah same here. Shame it's under these circumstances."

"Yeah, it really sucks, man. Bob was a good guy," Marco said, Brad, Susan and the others all agreeing.

They made small talk for an hour, then a man Ray didn't know, but said he was Bob's cousin, asked everyone to take a seat and he said a few words about Bob, how tragic his death was and that Bob was now in a better place.

Ray listened to it all, highly doubting Bob was anywhere better than being alive. He got to talk to Susan for a bit and she hugged him when she began to tear up at the loss of Bob. Though a sad occasion, he found his heart beating in excitement as he held her, smelling her hair, the softness of her beautiful neck so close. He'd almost leaned in and kissed the nape of her neck but had come to his senses at the last second. No, he'd told himself. Susan was with Brad. They were happy together. He needed to drop this infatuation with her or he would end up dying alone.

When the wake ended, Ray said goodbye to everyone and explained that he couldn't be at the funeral the next day due to work, Mary also saying she wasn't able to come.

"That's okay, Ray," Brad said. "You came tonight, that's what matters."

A few more goodbyes were made and Ray left. On the drive home, he couldn't help but think about Bob, how the man was the same age as him and he'd died of a heart attack. Ray made a resolve to appreciate life just a little bit more. After all, you never knew when it was your time to go.

The months passed quickly, as they always did, and by July, Ray had been in and out of a relationship with a co-worker. She'd told him it wasn't working out, that whenever he looked at her, it was like he was seeing someone else in her eyes. Ray knew she was right. Susan was always on his mind, and no matter how much he tried to forget her, he just couldn't.

Then, on the morning of July third, at three o'clock in the morning, he got a phone call that had him up for the rest of the night. It was Susan. She'd called to tell him that Marco was dead, a victim of a mugging gone wrong earlier that night when he had been out clubbing in the city with some friends and had gone off alone for a few minutes to take a leak in an alley. The wake was in two days, maybe three; she would call with more information when she had it. She'd gotten the notification from Marco's sister, who was taking it very hard. Marco had a large family and he was well-liked by all who knew him. The wake would be very busy, Susan was sure of it.

Ray had hung up and stared at the wall, then had gotten up to use the bathroom and get a drink of water.

It had taken infinitely long for the sun to rise as the hours passed from night to day.

Marco's wake and funeral came and went and life got back to normal for Ray. Work kept him busy and the days flew by. Before he realized it, Christmas had come and gone and it was the day of

New Year's Eve. He was excited about that night. Susan and Brad were having their annual party and he was looking forward to seeing her again.

It had been a rough year for all of them, what with the death of Bob and Marco, both their passings sudden and shocking. But Ray's father used to say that when it was your time, it was your time, and no mater what you did or didn't do, it didn't matter. When the good Lord wanted to take you, He would.

Finally that night arrived and Ray entered Brad and Susan's house a little after ten p.m. Susan saw him enter and went to him immediately, giving him a big hug. He tried not to think about how her breasts felt pressed against him and how her hair smelled as it tickled his cheek. He could have stayed that way forever, but then Brad walked up and Ray disengaged himself. He felt like Brad was seeing right through him, that he knew of Ray's inner feelings for his wife, but if he did, Brad didn't show any signs.

"Ray, it's good to see you, man," Brad said and shook his hand.

"Same here, how've you been since Marco's funeral?" Ray asked.

Brad shrugged. "About the same." He gestured to the empty living room, decorated with streamers and *Happy New Year* signs. "As you can see, you're the first one to get here. Mary and Rick are running late I guess."

Ray glanced at his wristwatch. It was going on half past ten. He was a few minutes late himself actually. Susan had told him to arrive by ten. "Well, there is some traffic like there is every New Year's Eve," he said and walked with the couple to the table set up with alcohol to get a drink.

Susan nodded. "I suppose, but usually those two are early." Then she waved her concerns away. "I'm just being paranoid, what with everything that's happened over the past year. It seems like our little group is dropping like flies."

Ray didn't have an answer for that, but merely sipped his drink, a specialty of Brad's, filled with Rum, Vodka and grenadine. They all walked over to the couch and sat down.

"Now, Susan," Brad said, "that's crazy talk. We've been over this before. Bob and Marco dying was a tragedy but purely a coincidence that they knew one another. Bob died of a heart attack and Marco a mugging. The two things couldn't be more distant from one another."

"I heard a story once about this guy who fell overboard on a cruise ship," Ray began, getting the married couple's attention. "He was drunk when he fell over and when he hit the water and went under, he thought he was dead. But he missed getting chewed up by the giant propellers and swam to the surface. Though he yelled for help, the ship was soon gone. He floated for three days in that cold ocean water and on the third day, dehydrated and exhausted, with no help in sight, he'd decided it was time to give up. He was going to just sink and drown and end his suffering. But just before he was going to do it, a fishing trawler appeared on the horizon, slowly moving closer, but not exactly to his location. He began screaming as hard as he could, waving his arms, and you know what? Someone on the main deck happened to spot him from the trawler and the boat headed for him. They pulled him out and he was saved."

"Shit," Brad said, "that was one lucky bastard."

"I know, right?" Ray agreed. "What I got from the story was that the guy never should have lived through that. He should have drowned, or been chewed up by the propellers, or sharks could have gotten to him, or even just becoming too tired to remain afloat and drowned, not to mention hyperthermia. But the guy avoided all that and a one in a million chance of a boat coming by in the middle of the ocean happened and saved his butt. And you know why he didn't die?"

Both Susan and Brad shook their heads.

"Because it wasn't his time, that's why. His number wasn't up so he lived, while other people step off the curb on their way to work and get hit by a bus, or they're working out at the gym and are in perfect health, but then suddenly drop dead from a blood clot or an aneurism."

"Not bad, Ray, that's a hell of a story. Kind of puts it all in perspective," Brad said.

"Maybe so, but I'm calling Rick and then Mary to see where they are." Susan went to her cell phone, dialed, and after a few minutes returned to Brad and Ray, who had been talking about the Red Sox and their team's chances the coming Spring.

"I called them both and both calls went to voice mail." She looked concerned.

"Oh, honey," Brad said, putting an arm around her. "They're probably at his or her place hooking up and that's why they aren't answering their phones. They'll be here, just give it time."

"I suppose you're right. Those two have been F-buddies for as long as we've known them."

"I know," Ray agreed. "It's funny how they never became an actual couple."

"No reason to," Brad replied. "And why would Rick bother anyway? He gets to have sex whenever he wants and doesn't have to deal with the rest of the shit that comes with a relationship."

Susan punched his arm. "Hey, that's not funny."

Brad smirked. "No, of course not, Suz, I was only joking." He gestured to the table filled with alcohol. "Would you mind getting me another drink? And Ray could use a top off."

She frowned but did as asked. When she was gone, Brad patted Ray's arm and said, "I wasn't joking, buddy. Sometimes, the extra shit that comes with a relationship can get mighty heavy."

Ray only nodded as he watched Susan walk away, admiring her trim figure. He swore she looked better every year. Brad kept talking about how marriage could be a drag and how it would be nice to be a free man again. Ray nodded and sipped his drink, the corner of his eyes on Susan the entire time. He watched the way she poured the drinks, the way her hair flowed over her shoulders, and his heart swelled with the love he'd had for her since high school. Though he acted like he agreed with Brad, deep in his heart, he knew that if he had been lucky enough to have gotten Susan for his own instead of Brad, he doubted very much that he wouldn't have been the happiest man on Earth.

Rick and Mary never showed for the party, and two days later Ray got a phone call that was hard to listen to.

From what Brad told Ray on the call, and from what Brad had learned from Mary's father when the man had answered Mary's cell phone, after days of Brad and Susan calling her as well as Rick, that both Mary and Rick had been in the same car on New Year's Eve, on their way to Susan and Brad's party, when a drunk driver had jumped the medium and had hit them head on going seventy.

Both of them died on impact, two more fatalities in the drunk driving list of deaths that grew every year.

Ray had listened to more as Brad explained what time exactly and where it had happened but Ray had barely listened. Two more of his friends were now dead and it was hard to take in. Ray heard Brad tell him he would let him know when and where the wakes and funerals for both Mary and Rick were being held when the news came in. Ray had grunted in reply and hung up.

Though he'd never been very close to either Rick or Mary, the idea that they were now dead was still a sobering thought. Though acquaintances, he still cared for them and of course wouldn't want anything bad to happen to either of them. The idea that they died on New Year's Eve while he, Brad and Susan drank and laughed made him feel even more guilty.

But there was nothing he could do about it, so though feeling unsettled, he returned to his day, knowing he would once more have to attend more funerals.

But there was a bright side to it all, as morbid as it sounded.

He would get to see Susan again.

Mary's funeral was rough for Ray, despite him not being very close to her. Mary had a large family that had loved her very much, and between her parents crying and her three brothers, the entire affair had gotten quite emotional.

Ray had been thankful when she was in the ground and he was able to put the terrible experience behind him.

But no sooner did Mary's funeral end than Rick's began. Luckily, there was no wake for Rick for reasons he didn't care to hear about, but the funeral was much longer than others he'd attended. Rick had been Catholic so first everyone went to the church where there was a special Mass for him, then everyone went to the cemetery to bury his casket and finally, everyone who attended was invited to Rick's parent's home for refreshments. Ray might have passed on this but after spending half the day putting Rick in the ground, he was starving and a free meal seemed like the perfect thing to salvage the day.

Brad and Susan had been at the funeral, too, but there had been no time for Ray to talk to either of them, though he had snuck many private glances at Susan, who looked stunning in a simple black dress and matching shoes. Brad, like Ray, had worn a dark suit.

It was while they were eating from a buffet-style spread that Susan, Brad and Ray finally got a chance to talk.

"I want to show you something, Ray," Susan said and handed him a piece of paper across from the table they were sitting at. Other mourners were eating nearby, but not where they were sitting. Rick's parents owned a large mansion in the suburbs, and the main room was large enough to fit double the size of people now in it.

"Oh come on, Susan, not this again," Brad said and tried to take the paper from her before she could give it to Ray. She yanked her hand back and he missed.

"No, Brad," she said, adamant. "This is real, I'm telling you this is real."

"What are you two arguing about?" Ray asked as he chewed what remained of half of a stuffed shell filled with ricotta cheese. The buffet was filled with pastas, deli platters and pastries. If it wasn't such a morose occasion, Ray would have loved every minute of the magnificent layout of food.

Susan leaned over the table and practically shoved the paper she was holding at Ray. "Here, take this," she demanded. "I found it when I was cleaning the other day. It was stuffed in a desk drawer."

He did, and after wiping his mouth on a cloth napkin, he looked at the paper and what it contained. "What is this?"

"Don't you remember?" she asked.

Ray shook his head. "Should I?"

"It's that list of dates we got from that website last year," Brad explained. "Remember?" Brad asked. "Bob had us go onto that death site and we typed in our socials and got what was supposed to be our time of deaths. It was all just a big joke."

"No, it wasn't a joke, dammit," Susan growled. "Ray, look at the dates for Bob, Marco, Mary and Rick, then tell me it's all a joke. Tell me those dates aren't the exact dates they died."

Ray began reading each date, that night coming back to him. He thought back to Bob's death and when it happened, then Marco's. The dates were the same. And now Mary and Rick, both on the same day, New Year's Eve. He thought back to how they had joked about them both getting the same expiration date and had made a big joke about it. But here it was a week after the thirty-first and they were dead, both at the same time, in the same car. His mind raced with the idea that the website had been real, that it truly told a person when they would die.

But of course that was ridiculous. No one knew when they were going to die, that was impossible, not if you were healthy and fit. Sure, maybe if a person had cancer or some life-threatening illness, but even then, their death was never exact, but only a general timeline, whether weeks or months. But a perfectly healthy person? How could someone know they would be in a car accident? Or get shot, or have a heart attack when they were perfectly fine?

Ray put the paper down and shoved some salad with vinaigrette dressing into his mouth. "Brad's right. It's not possible. It has to be some kind of sick coincidence."

"I don't think it was," she replied. "If you look at the dates again…"

"Enough, Susan, you need to stop this," Brad said, sounding angry. "We've already talked about this and you said you weren't going to do this here."

"Well, I changed my mind. Ray has a right to know, too." Her voice went up a little as she tried to make her point.

Ray and Brad shared gazes and Ray saw Brad shrug with a *wives, what are you gonna do?*

"And I thank you, Susan. But I really don't think this is relevant," Ray said, trying to calm her down. She was looking more upset and had already elicited a few concerned glances, people wanting to know what was going on; why she was being so loud.

"Okay, Susan, you said your peace, I think we should go now," Brad said. He stood up and began making Susan stand, too.

"No, Brad, Ray needs to listen to me. This list is real, that site knows the truth."

"Sure it does," Brad said. His eyes went to Ray and Ray could see the embarrassment there. "We're gonna go now, Susan's had enough for one day."

"But you don't understand!" Susan yelled. "It's all true, all of it. Damn it, listen to me!"

Brad led Susan through the house, telling a few people close by that she was upset about Rick's death. No one seemed to mind, as each person grieved in their own way. A few minutes later, Brad and Susan were gone and the disruption was forgotten as soon as it had begun.

Ray felt so bad for Susan, wondering what was wrong with her. As he reached for his drink, his eyes went to the paper still on the table, where Susan had left it in the commotion. He picked it up again and studied the dates.

A soft voice in the back of his head began to get louder. What if Susan was right? What if the dates were correct and somehow that website knew your time of death? If it was true, would he, Ray, want to know his death? Would that be a good thing or a bad thing? After all, if he knew when he was going to die, he could make sure he did all the things he wanted to do before his time came, and then he could get his affairs in order. But to know when he as a person, as a human being, would cease, right down to the day, well, that would be a heavy weight to have on one's shoulders. Maybe it wouldn't be a good thing.

He read the remaining dates of those in their group that were still alive. Brad Susan and Ray were all that was left. So if this was true, then Brad had until 9/15/16. That was years away. Susan's was two years after that and if this was all true, then Ray had the longest to live.

At least he could take heart in that.

Then he discarded the notion as ludicrous, but he didn't toss the paper back on the table. Instead, he folded it neatly and put it into his pocket. After that, any more thought on the subject was over when Rick's father walked up to him and they began to talk.

Soon, the entire time of death thing was forgotten.

The next three years passed as they always do, far too fast.

No more New Year's Eve parties were held at Susan's house. After the death of Rick and Mary, it just didn't seem right, especially since it was now the anniversary of their deaths. Ray lost touch with Susan and Brad without even realizing it, his own life keeping him busy.

He'd met a few women over the years, but nothing had ever become serious. Though he didn't talk to her anymore, Susan was always in the back of his mind. A few times he'd thought of contacting her, but had stopped himself at the last second. He knew he needed to let go, that the love he had for her could never be, and he was going to die a hermit if he didn't accept this.

So to say he was shocked, pleased and surprised to get a call from her out of the blue in September would be an understatement. The second he heard her voice and she said it was her, his heart skipped a beat in joy, but then he picked up on her tone of her voice, the hitch in her throat as she tried not to cry, the sense of grief filling her.

"What's wrong? Are you okay?" His joy had changed to one of concern in the blink of an eye.

"Oh Ray, it's…it's Brad."

"Brad? What's wrong with him. Is he all right?"

"No, Ray, he's dead, Brad is dead." She began to cry then, the dam bursting. Ray said nothing as he listened to her sobbing, his own mind racing with the idea. Though Brad and he had never been that close, it was still quite a shock.

"Stay there, I'm coming right over," Ray said.

Susan muttered something about how she wasn't leaving the house and Ray hung up.

He broke every traffic law getting to her.

"Tell me how it happened," Ray said as he sat next to Susan on the couch in her living room.

The date was September 16, 2016

Susan wiped her eyes and showed Ray a newspaper with yesterday's date. On the front page, off to the side, was a small byline: **Man killed in Ted Williams tunnel. Faulty ceiling the cause**.

Below that was the article explaining how a piece of the tunnel ceiling had given out thanks to water corrosion. A six foot slab of concrete had finally let go during rush hour and Brad had been the unlucky commuter to be under it when it did. The roof of his car was crushed with him inside it. He was pronounced dead on the scene.

Ray put the paper down. "Jesus Christ, I don't believe it." He had heard about the tunnel ceiling collapse while at work but he'd had no idea it had been Brad who was the victim. Perhaps if he'd watched the news yesterday, but he'd gotten in late and had gone right to bed. He'd missed the entire thing.

"Oh, Susan, I'm so sorry," he said and pulled her too him. She let him do this and her head went under his chin as she began to cry again.

He held her, rocking her gently, telling her how things would be okay. As he did this, his eyes went to the newspaper and the black and white picture of a car crushed under a slab of concrete. A one in a million chance of being the one to die in that accident. Thousands of people had been driving through the tunnel that day and the slab had picked that exact moment to let go, just as Brad went under it.

Ray heard a voice in his head: *When your number's up, your number's up.*

That was what had happened to Brad.

The next few days were crazy busy for Ray as he helped Susan deal with Brad's affairs, including the wake and funeral. Brad's parents also helped, but it was Ray that Susan seemed to lean on the most. Not that Ray minded. He was with her most of the time, having taken some time off work so he could be with her. He would sit and listen to her talk about Brad, how good he'd been to her.

Then, out of the blue, Susan brought up the paper with the death dates on them, asking Ray if he remembered when Brad's was. Ray told her no, not wanting to upset her. She had assumed she'd lost the paper back at Rick's funeral but Ray had kept it all this time, and when Susan had called and told him of Brad's death, he'd pulled it out of the folder it was stored in and was shocked to see that the date of Brad's death was September 15, 2016.

As he stared at the paper and the dates, he realized that so far, all five of his friends had died on the exact date foretold from the website. A small part of his mind yelled at him, told him he was being silly, that there was no way this could be true, but as time went by and he thought more about it, he knew he had to accept reality for what it was. What was the other saying his father used to use? If it walks like a duck and quacks like a duck, then it's a *fucking* duck. His old man had added the curse word to make the saying his own, and Ray had always chuckled upon hearing it. His mother had always frowned deeply.

But even if the dates were real, Susan had two years before her time was up. Ray still had two years to be with her, and knowing this, he decided not to waste one more minute without her. Now that Brad was gone, it was his chance to be with her. Of course he would wait a decent time before asking her out, and even then he still might be moving too fast if she was still grieving, but he would take it slow and see when she looked ready.

That was exactly what Ray did.

Over the next year, he spent a lot of time with Susan. He would always be there when she called him for help, such as if she had a leaky kitchen sink or the toilet wouldn't stop filling. He would spend Sundays with her, cutting the grass and having lunch, tuna being his favorite.

When it was almost exactly a year since Brad's passing, he made his move, telling her that he loved her and had for pretty much his entire life, or since high school anyway. At first she'd been taken aback, and had said only a year passing since Brad's death was too soon for her. Ray had told her it was fine, that he was willing to wait as long as it took, though deep down he prayed she would be his one day. By this time, he'd almost completely forgotten about the paper with the death dates on them. For the first time in a long while, he was happy, and even if they had to stay apart as far as dating, as long as he was able to see and be with her, he was a happy man.

Another month passed and Ray found himself staying well past dinner time one night. He was sitting on the couch, sipping the glass of wine she'd given him. Susan had left the room to go into the rear of the house, where her bedroom was. Ray hadn't given it much thought until she'd come back into the living room wearing a black negligee that was almost see-thru. Her hair had been styled and it draped over her shoulders, her face glowing.

"It's time," she'd said simply. "It's been long enough. I know Brad would want me to be happy and he always liked you. I have to believe he would approve of us." She'd then turned and walked away, her footsteps telling him she was going to her bedroom again.

With butterflies in his stomach, Ray had downed the rest of the wine in his glass, poured himself another, and promptly downed that as well.

Then he'd turned off the television, gathered his courage, unable to believe his wish was finally coming true, and walked down the hallway to the bedroom.

Susan was waiting for him in the bed, one leg propped up seductively, her back arced like a siren, the lights turned down low. She gestured for him to come closer.

Ray crossed the room and fell into her arms.

It was one of the most wonderful nights of his entire life; even the best times with his ex-wife and the few flings he'd had could not compare to making love to Susan.

As for her, at first she was tense, as if she was having second thoughts about what she was doing, but as the night passed and they made love for the third and fourth times, Susan finally gave into her lust and passion.

And Ray was finally able to release all the pent-up love he'd had for her.

That night two became one and she fell in love with Ray.

They married three months later, though Susan thought it was a little fast. But Ray convinced her there was no need to wait. They had known each other for more than twenty years, what did a few more months of dating matter?

They went to Hawaii for their honeymoon and had a wonderful time. When they returned, Ray gave up his apartment and moved in with her. He thought it would have been a little uncomfortable being there, thinking Brad's ghost would always be hovering over him, haunting him, but it wasn't like that at all.

One day, when he was checking the calendar for when they could take a vacation, thoughts of the death website arose in his mind. But no sooner did the images of names and dates appear, then he forced them back down.

No, he thought. He was happy with her, had finally found the peace he'd wanted since high school. He refused to let it be sullied by something that might not even happen.

As the months passed, he slowly managed to convince himself that it had all been a horrible dream, and that the sequence of deaths had been a terrible coincidence.

There were always voices in the back of his mind telling him he was wrong, that he was just telling himself what he wanted to hear, but he ignored those voices, wanting to be happy.

He had to do this, for the alternative was too much to contemplate.

Time zipped by and sometimes he couldn't believe how happy he was. Susan was too. Though she missed Brad, she had fallen in love with Ray and was glad to have a second chance at love. Ray, not being selfish, was never upset if she brought up Brad, and there were times the two would lay in bed together and she would talk about Brad, sharing memories of all the good times she'd had with him. Ray didn't mind sharing her with Brad's memory for in the end, the man was dead and she was in his arms each night.

She was his.

One time she tried to bring up the death dates but Ray had quickly changed the subject, and before Susan realized it, they were talking about something entirely different. This happened on more than one occasion and later, as they either lay in bed or sat together on the couch, with her curled up beside him, Ray's face would take on one of worry as he considered those fateful dates and the one slowly approaching that could mean the death of Susan.

Each New Year's Eve was now spent with just the two of them, and Ray had to admit that was the way he liked it.

But no matter how much he wanted time to stand still, it wouldn't, and usually ended up moving even faster. Before Ray knew it, it was August 23, 2018.

He stayed home from work that day, too fearful to leave Susan alone. He doted over her all day and drove her crazy, never letting her out of his sight. Those voices in his head were loud now, telling him that this was the day. If the death site had been real, if it really, *really* had been able to foretell the future, this would be the day the woman he loved would die.

He was a nervous wreck the entire day, always keeping his eyes out for something that could hurt Susan. He also knew that from the others that had died, it wasn't necessarily an outside influence that could kill her. For all he knew, even staying in the house was dangerous. A plane could fall out of the sky, the gas main could have a leak and explode. He constantly checked all these things, monitoring the news and running around the house,

Susan thinking her husband was going crazy. He tried not to think she could have a heart attack like Bob, for there was no way he could prevent that.

Finally, a little after nine that night, after he'd kept her from going shopping, going for a walk, and even going outside in the backyard earlier, she confronted him in the living room.

"All right, mister, that's it. I can't take this anymore." Her arms were crossed over her chest, a sign to Ray that she meant business. "You've been acting crazy all day. Now you tell me what's going on or so help me I'm leaving this house right now and there's nothing you can do to stop me unless you try and physically hold me down." Her face took on a look of defiance. "And I wouldn't recommend that if you cherish your balls in one piece."

He might have tried to physically stop her, but he could see it in her eyes that the jig was up. He could either tell her what day it was or do something to distract her, which by the way she was looking at him, he doubted it would work. But he had one more trick up his sleeve and he played it now.

He did the only thing he could; he asked her to go out to dinner and a movie to distract her, which she quickly said yes, feeling slightly stir crazy from being inside all day. Besides, if it was nine at night and she was fine. What could happen in three more hours? So the site really was silly and most definitely not true...thank God.

She changed into a nice dress and Ray did the same, getting out of his sweatpants and into a nice pair of slacks and a dress shirt. Then they left the house and into the night. Ray made sure she wore her seatbelt and he drove like an old man, Susan annoyed by it, but they reached the restaurant safely and the dinner went smoothly. From there they walked to the movie house which was only two blocks over. Ray always kept Susan near the buildings and his eyes scanned his surrounding like a hawk, looking up, and side to side. No brick was going to dislodge from a building and hit her on the head, or car swerve onto the sidewalk and hit her.

The movie was a Romcom and Ray had to admit he would have liked it if he could have concentrated on it for more than two seconds. Even in the movie house he was constantly watching others, as if he was a bodyguard on detail.

The movie ended and they left, shuffling out with the other patrons. Once on the street, they began their walk back to Ray's parked car.

Ray made sure they stayed in well-lit areas with other people about, not wanting to take the chance of getting mugged, and no doubt Susan being killed in the incident.

They were halfway there when Susan suddenly stopped and Ray, realizing she wasn't with him, panicked and spun around, about to run after her, but then he halted suddenly upon seeing she was right behind him.

"There," she said. "There it is again. You're like a frightened cat in a room full of dogs. You've been on edge all night. Tell me what's the matter with you? And no more lies and changing the subject."

He sighed heavily, wanting to tell her but hesitating. She could see he had something on his chest so she prodded him some more.

"Come on, spill it, tell me what's got you so concerned that you've been hovering over me like a mother hen all day?" She crossed her arms over her chest and he saw her wristwatch peeking out of her sleeve. He also saw it was only a minute to midnight. Sixty seconds more and the curse was over, the thing he'd been worrying about for almost a year put behind him…finally.

It was time to come clean, nothing could happen in less than a minute.

"Okay, I'll tell you because it doesn't matter anymore. In a few seconds it'll be midnight and a new day." He hesitated for a heartbeat and said, "Today was the day you were supposed to die. It was the date on that paper you gave me from that death website."

"No kidding?" Her eyes went wide.

"Yup, but we've proved it was all a lie. It's midnight of the next day and you're still here with me. I've been worried about it for all this time for nothing. Bob, Marco, Brad, the others, it was all a coincidence, though a terrible one. I knew it was, too, but I let my stupid superstitious nature get the best of me."

She checked her watch and it was now a minute past midnight. She laughed, her voice strong and full of joy, of life. "It's the next day. I'm still here. It was all false. I'm still here!" She laughed louder and jumped into his arms and they kissed, tears of joy falling down his cheeks.

"You're crying," she said and wiped his cheeks with her finger.

"I thought I was going to lose you today. I feel so foolish now." He hugged her so hard she slapped his arms to make him let her go.

"I can't breathe, let me go," she gasped and he did just that. Then she looked around them and realized something. "Hey, aren't we going the wrong way? I thought we parked at the garage on North St."

"Hey, you're right. Shit, I was so preoccupied I was taking us to the wrong garage. I use the one we were going to sometimes when I have to park around here when I run errands during my lunch hour at work."

They began walking back the way they'd come, Susan leading the way. Ray was fine with this. It was the next day after all, all was well. At the corner, Susan stepped off the curb, but as she did, she had turned slightly so she could look at Ray, wanting to blow him a kiss. In that exact moment, to Ray, she looked absolutely beautiful. There was a lamp post over her and the light shone down on her, her flawless skin seeming to glow. Her lips still had on the red lipstick she'd applied after dinner and her lips seemed to float on her face, as she puckered to blow him that kiss.

Their eyes met for that moment, and in that glance, all the love he felt for her was returned ten fold, and he knew he couldn't have been happier if money had begun to fall from the sky.

And that was when a transit bus came roaring around the corner, the off-duty driver in a rush to get back to the depot, his shift over. It had been a long day and he wanted to go home, have a beer and go to bed, so he was driving way over the speed limit, assuming at midnight the streets were relatively empty.

Susan's gaze was locked on Ray as the bus hit her at over fifty miles an hour, knocking her down and then running over her body, which became mangled beneath the undercarriage of the roaring bus. She was knocked up and down like a child's toy, then spit out the back end of the bus as if she was a half-eaten piece of food being spit out of a fussy diner's mouth at a high-priced restaurant. The bus driver began screaming when he realized he'd hit a person, and swerved hard to the right and hit a parked car. The sound of rending meal and smashing glass filled the street.

At first Ray didn't move, frozen at the sight before him, but as the seconds ticked by, he went into action.

"Noooo! Susan, noooo!" he yelled, running full tilt to her bloody and still form now laying in the middle of the street. There was a smear of blood behind her from where she'd been dragged, before popping out of the back of the bus, to roll twice and lay still. She was lying on her back, her head turned to the side, a jagged bone sticking out of her throat. Both arms were broken, one leg bent almost backwards, the white of more bone poking through her shredded flesh.

Her eyes were open but they saw nothing, she was already dead.

"This can't be happening! It was past the day! It was the next day. She made it through her date!" Ray screamed as he dropped down beside her, the knees of his pants immediately becoming soaked in her spilled blood. He wanted to pick her up, cradle her to him, but he stopped, not wanting to touch her, afraid she would fall apart if he moved her. The smell of blood and shit filled his nostrils and he leaned to the side and threw up his dinner, his hacking replaced by sobbing intermittently.

All around him people were gathering, most with cell phones to their ears to call for help, but he barely saw any of this. His attention was only on his late wife, the woman he'd loved for what seemed to him like forever.

As he leaned over her, caressing her face, closing her eyes so he didn't have to stare at those blank orbs, his gaze went down to her left arm. Her wristwatch was still there, still working. He'd given it to her a few months ago as a present and had bragged how it was impact resistant. The time read four minutes past midnight.

His own shirtsleeve was pulled up as he leaned over her and his wristwatch was also visible to him, and as his eyes flicked from hers to his and then back again, he realized that they weren't in synch, that hers was in fact running five minutes faster than his.

Ray's watch said it was still one minute to midnight, which made no sense.

And then he remembered with horror that she always set her watch five minutes fast so she wouldn't be late for appointments.

Thinking back to only minutes ago, he realized that he had only looked at her watch when she'd crossed her arms before her when they were talking, and he'd totally forgotten that hers was running fast, which meant that at that precise moment, it had still been August twenty-third.

Reality struck him like a ton of bricks, already flattening his devastated soul, and he came to the conclusion that the death site was absolutely and completely real, that each date foretold was in fact the date of a person's death. Susan's death had proved this without a doubt. She had died on the day she was fated to; there had been one more minute left until midnight.

Though Ray struggled to stay conscious, it was all too much and he fainted, collapsing on his dead love.

Ray was never the same after Susan's death.

It wasn't long before he lost his job and began to drink heavily to dull the pain.

Only his own savings complied with what Susan had in the bank and the life insurance she had allowed him to keep a roof over his head and not lose the house he and Susan once shared.

The next three years passed in a blur of alcohol fueled nightmares where he saw Susan being hit over and over again, a movie set to rewind on one particular spot for all eternity.

For he now believed with all his heart that he would die on April 21, 2021—which was tomorrow.

The living room was almost completely dark, only one small lamp in the corner allowing Ray to see by. On the couch beside him was his and Susan's wedding picture, the photo now crusted with dirt from all the times he'd handled it with dirty hands. It didn't matter, nothing did.

Knowing it would only be April twentieth for a few more minutes, he made sure to have a full bottle of Jack Daniels on the coffee table before him, as he sat on his filthy couch and watched the minute hand on the wall-clock slowly move around until it was 11:59 in tandem with the second hand.

He planned on being good and drunk real soon, if that was even possible after the amount of alcohol he'd consumed over the past few years.

When that second hand struck midnight along with the minute hand, it would be his day to die. He didn't know how it would happen, but he knew with every fiber of his being that it would.

There was no way to stop it, there was nowhere he could go to hide; there was nothing he could do but accept it.

Sitting silently, he waited as the second hand began its final circle to midnight.

BLACK EASTER

CHRISTOPHER BECK

"Get down from there, Beau," Brianna said. "We can't peek."

Beau, with his tongue dangling from his mouth and his tail wagging, was standing on his hind legs, looking out the window.

At the mention of his name, the dog looked over at Brianna and then back out the window.

"I know you're excited," Brianna said. "I am, too. But we have to wait for Mommy to finish hiding the eggs. And we can't peek, so come here."

It was Easter Sunday, the eighth for Brianna and the first for her Shih Tzu.

Despite the bright sun sitting proudly in the sky, watching the world below, the afternoon was chilly. A light breeze did nothing to help, but it didn't matter; the chill, try as it might, couldn't take away from the excitement.

Beau stood his ground at the window. Brianna, who was sitting in the middle of the living room floor with her brightly-colored basket next to her, patted her lap and called him again. This time Beau obeyed.

He dropped from the window, ran to Brianna, jumped in her lap, and began to lick her face.

The doggy kisses tickled Brianna's face but she let them continue. She laughed, and then said, "I love you, too, you fuzzy muppet." She ruffled Beau's brown and white fur with both of her hands and kissed him back.

The two kept tickling and kissing each other until they heard the back door open and close a few moments later. Together they both sat, eyes and ears open, waiting for Brianna's mother to pop around the corner of the laundry room.

After the door closed the trailer remained silent. There were no footfalls, and after a few seconds, Brianna, feeling a pang of worry, said, "Mom?"

No answer, no movement, no noise.

"Mommy?" Brianna questioned again. She hugged Beau tighter to her chest. The worry pang was starting to form into something bigger.

Then, Brianna's mom, with a bunny mask on her head, hopped around the corner playfully and yelled, "Happy Easter!"

Happy to see her, Beau squirmed out of Brianna's arms and ran to Mom. Brianna, relief easing her gooseflesh, stood and followed him. "God, Mom. You scared me."

Mom laughed as she pulled the mask off. She tossed it on the kitchen table and gave Brianna a hug. "Sorry 'bout that, honey," she said with a smile. "I couldn't resist. The eggs are all hidden. Are you two ready?"

"Yes, yes!" Brianna cried happily.

"All right," Mom said as she let Brianna go. "Get a jacket on and get your basket."

"Yippee!" Brianna yelled as she turned and hurried to her room. She wasted no time in getting her jacket, and taking her basket in her other hand on the way back to the kitchen. "Ready, Mom," she said upon arriving.

Beau smiled, panted and wagged his tail as Mom clipped his leash on.

"I think Beau is ready, too," Mom said.

"Yea, I'd say so," Brianna said. She bent down and patted Beau on the head. "Are you ready for your first Easer Egg hunt, huh? Are you ready?"

"All right," Mom said. "Let's get to it."

"Yay," Brianna said while clapping. She jumped up and down in anticipation. "How many eggs did you hide, Mommy?"

"Twenty-four," Mom said.

"Wow, that's a lot," Brianna said with wide eyes.

The three of them walked out the back door.

The yard around the single-wide trailer home wasn't big by any standards but that didn't bother Brianna. It was big enough for her to have fun. The giant smile on her face seemed permanent and that made Mom smile.

Brianna took the lead, followed by Mom and Beau. "Come on, Beau," Brianna said. "Help me find some eggs."

Beau looked at Brianna and then looked away.

"Some help you are," Brianna said in a huff.

The eggs that Mom hid were plastic ones filled with various candies or money, both paper and coins. The first one Brianna found was green and it rattled when she picked it up. Before she put it in her basket, she gave it a shake and said, "It's money."

"Hold it up," Mom said. She slipped the loop at the end of the dog leash around her wrist, powered up her camera. "Say Happy Easter!"

"Happy Easter," Brianna yelled. "Oh, take one of me and Beau. Come here, Beau." She knelt down and picked up the dog when he came to her. "Smile and say Happy Easter!"

"Okay," Mom said, "now go find some more eggs."

Brianna giggled and put Beau down, then turned and resumed the hunt. She quickly found a second egg, then a third. Mom followed behind her and snapped pictures. Beau was rolling around in the grass behind Mom.

None of the small, happy family saw or heard the pit bull until it was too late. A tug on the leash, and an ear-piercing, heart-breaking yelp shattered the serenity of the afternoon and killed the family's excitement.

Brianna and Mom both jumped at the sound and turned to see a gray pit bull toss Beau up into the air by its mouth, only to catch him again. Beau's brown fur was already stained with blood.

Brianna dropped the egg she was holding in her hand, as tears blurred her vision and fear stole her voice. Her heart rate instantly doubled and she found it was hard to take a breath.

Mom dropped her camera and felt the same things Brianna did.

She wanted to pull on the leash and yank Beau free, but knew it would do more harm than good. "Brianna, get in the house!"

Brianna stood, frozen.

Beau continued to cry out in pain. Blooded dripped from his body.

"Brianna, get in the house, now!"

This time Brianna did what she was told. Her legs felt like rubber as she ran, and thankfully she was still near the back door of the trailer and she didn't have to run far.

She ran up the steps, yanked the door open, slammed it behind her, dropped her basket, ran over to the kitchen window, and looked out.

She began to cry, and for the first time in her young life she'd experienced true horror.

Mom did the first thing that came to mind. She rushed over to the pit bull and kicked it in its side but it barely noticed the blow so she bent down, grabbed the dog's upper and lower jaws, and tried to pry them open.

She had to save her pet, what to her was like a second child.

The pit bull, not liking the placement of Mom's hands, lashed out with one of its paws. The claws tore into Mom's skin just above the wrist and drew blood.

Beau's cries tapered off and became whimpers.

Mom ignored the fiery pain in her arm and kept pulling. Finally, whether she had pulled the jaws apart or the pit bull simply had let go, Beau's battered and bloodied body fell free of the dog's mouth.

The pit bull snapped at Mom as she snatched Beau up off the ground; luckily its teeth only grazed the back of her hand. She stood, introduced the tip of her shoe to the pit bull's nose, then turned and fled into the house.

"Brianna!" Mom called out as she slammed the door closed behind her. "Get me some towels!"

Brianna hurried to the bathroom and returned with two beach towels.

"Set them on the table," Mom said.

Brianna did so and Mom carefully put Beau on the towels and wrapped the dog up.

"Is…is…he going to be okay, Mom?" Brianna asked, her voice timid.

"I don't know, honey," Mom said. She wanted to hug Brianna but the bloodstains on her shirt kept her from doing so. "We have to get him to a vet. Grab my pocketbook, my keys are in there and my wallet."

Brianna ran off and was back in seconds. Then they went out the front door to get to Mom's Ranger. Brianna got in and Mom put Beau on her lap.

"You're going to have to hold him," Mom said. "We have to keep him as still and comfortable as possible."

Brianna nodded and looked down at Beau. The dog's breathing was ragged and shallow, and only his eyes moved. They were filled with fear, like Brianna's, and to her it seemed like the life in them was fading. Brianna wiped her wet cheeks with the palm of her hand and continued to sob.

Mom closed Brianna's door and went around to the driver's side, and just as she was about to pull it open, she heard a deep growl from off to the side.

She quickly looked to see the pit bull coming around the front of the trailer, its mouth covered in blood—Beau's blood. Mom jumped in the Ranger and slammed the door a second before the pit bull jumped at the side of the vehicle.

It snapped at Mom's window, streaking it with salvia that had traces of red in it.

Mom wished she had a gun as she wiped tears from her cheeks, started the truck, and drove away.

I was at my oldest brother's, getting ready to have Easter dinner with him and his family when I got the call. My cell reception in his house is slim to none, so I stepped outside.

"Hello?" I said.

As soon as my ex-wife began to talk I knew something was wrong. Her voice was monotone and her nose sounded stuffy, and she kept sniffling. In the background, I could hear my step-daughter, Brianna, sobbing. I was instantly filled with dread.

"What's wrong, Lisa?" I asked.

Lisa told me about what had happened.

"The vet office in Millville was closed," she said. "We're on our way up to the Animal Hospital in Blackwood now."

Blackwood is a good hour away from where she was.

"No other place is open today?" I asked.

"No," Lisa said. "I was told that's the closest one there is."

"Where's Beau now?" I knew her truck was small.

"He's on Brianna's lap," she said.

The image of a terrified Brianna with her dying dog in her lap filled my mind. I bit my lip and sighed. I wished I was there to offer comfort.

"Can I talk to her?" I asked.

"Sure, Rob, hold on," Lisa said, and handed the phone over.

"Hello?" Brianna said. The hurt and fear in her voice was crushing.

"Hey, sweet pea," I said. "You okay?"

"No." Brianna's breath kept hitching as she sobbed and she kept sniffling to cut off her running nose.

Brianna recapped what had happened, and I let her. She needed to talk about it. Plus, I was at a loss for words. Aside from "I'm sorry," and "It's going to be okay," what else can one really say at a time like that?

"He whines whenever we hit a bump," Brianna said.

The two of us fell into a moment of silence. She asked if I wanted to talk to her mom again and I said I did. I told Brianna I loved her before she handed it back to Lisa.

"You know," I said, once Lisa was back on the phone. "They say that sometimes things happen for a reason. What happened is terrible, but if Beau wasn't there the pit bull might have come after you or Brianna."

"Yeah," Lisa said. She sniffled and I heard her take a deep drag on a cigarette.

We talked for a bit after that, mostly rehashing the same stuff. I told her to keep me posted and to let me know if she needed anything. She said she would.

A few hours later she called me back. She was just as upset as before.

"Beau's lungs are punctured, most of his ribs are broken, and his spine's damaged," Lisa said. "They said it'd be thousands of dollars to try and fix him. I don't have that kind of money."

I didn't either, but I wished I did. If it would have eased Lisa and Brianna's pain and brought their family back together, I would have given it up in a heartbeat.

"Rob, I told them to put him down," Lisa said. The words were not easy for her to speak.

"Oh man," I said. "That sucks."

"Yeah," Lisa agreed. "I'm going to take Brianna to her father's house and then I'm gonna go to the hospital to get my scratches and bite checked out. I don't want to risk getting rabies."

"That's a good idea," I said.

During the week that followed the attack, Lisa kept me up to date on what was going on. I even visited, hoping to offer whatever comfort I could. Lisa and Brianna were devastated to say the least, and Brianna was scared to go outside and each night she would wake up screaming.

The people of the mobile home community heard about what had happened and showed kindness by offering condolences and sending cards. It was touching. No one, however, could recall seeing a pit bull around before or after the attack. We were all outraged. The owner needed to be found and held accountable immediately.

Then there was a break-through, one that brought Lisa and Brianna some relief.

"We were getting out of the truck the next day," Lisa had told to me over the phone, "and this woman came walking up to me. I didn't know who she was and I'd never seen her before. Unsure of what was up, I told Brianna to go into the trailer."

"Okay," I said.

"She said her name was Allison and that she lived two trailers down, the last one on this road," Lisa explained. "She asked if I owned the dog that was attacked and I told her yes. Well, she said that the pit bull belonged to her and her boyfriend, Rich. On Easter they were going to her mother's for dinner and Rich tied the dog up outside." Lisa took a deep breath. "You're not supposed to tie up any animals around here; it's against the park rules. Anyway, it got loose while they were in their trailer getting ready. They noticed it was missing when they came back out but didn't go out looking for it, not wanting to be late for dinner."

"Jesus," I said. "They just left?"

"I know, I can't believe it either, Rob," Lisa said. "But it gets better."

"Do tell," I said.

"Well," Lisa continued, "she said that some time ago the pit bull ate one of the cats they had, and it bit her niece when her sister came to visit a while ago."

"And the sister didn't say anything?"

"Oh, she did, and the dog was taken away by the city, but they got it back after filing an appeal?"

"How the hell did that happen?"

"Damn if I know," Lisa said. "I have a feeling Rich might know someone on the town council by the way she explained it, by the way she said they got the dog back."

"That's terrible," I said. "Who would want a dog like that anyway? And why was she telling you about it?"

"Stupid people don't think," Lisa said, "and I think she was high. Her eyes were glassy and she kept scratching at marks on her arm that looked like track marks."

"That's wonderful," I said, "and these people live two trailers down?"

"Uh-huh," Lisa said.

"What's happing now?"

"We're waiting for animal control to come and take the dog away again; hopefully they'll put it to sleep this time."

"Good," I said, but I knew that wasn't going to be enough for me. These people, these dope fiends, these people with no regard for others, had caused my ex-wife and step-daughter great pain, endangered their lives. Brianna now had to face death in all its ugly glory. Lisa said she was distraught and was scared that she was going to die next. The child was far too young to be worrying about such things.

As the anger filled me so that I was seeing red, I knew then and there that someone had to pay.

The next day I went to Allison and Rich's trailer, my anger so high I swear I saw red.

I knew Miss Shirley, the elderly woman who lived in the trailer between Allison's and Lisa's, from my time living with Lisa, always went for walks in the middle of the day, so I wasn't worried about her looking out a window and seeing me.

Lisa and Brianna, still a bit unsettled by the Black Easter, went to the park and after that were going to the movies.

I went around the block and stopped in front of Allison's and Rich's trailer, lucky to see that neither of them was home, then I checked my mirrors and surroundings to make sure the coast was clear. Once I was sure I was alone, I hopped out of my pickup truck and opened the back. A large black pit bull growled at me through his muzzle. He was a mean bastard and didn't care for me much; the feeling was mutual.

I named him 'Blackie,' and I pulled him across the sidewalk and around to the side of the trailer. He fought me the entire time, but I was determined. I tied his leash around the railing of the small back porch, pulled on a pair of gloves, and took a small, flathead screwdriver from my pocket. I used the screwdriver to pop the lock on the back door.

"Come on, Blackie," I said, pulling him up the steps and into the trailer. "You'll be among your own kind here shortly." I dragged him to the living room, lifted an end of the sofa, and looped the end of the heavy-duty leash around the short leg before setting it back down. "Now, be a good boy, I'll be back in a minute."

I left the trailer, got in my truck, and drove over to the newer section of the community. I parked on the side of the road in front of an empty lot, pulled on a hoodie, leaving the hood up, got out, and walked back to the trailer and entered it.

I didn't know how long Allison and Rich were going to be gone but I didn't care. I was going to wait regardless.

The trailer was disgusting; dishes were piled in the sink, ants searched the counters for food, the kitchen floor was in desperate need of a mopping, the filthy carpet was covered in cigarette burns, and a small square mirror and cut straws rested on the kitchen table, as did a pipe and a water bong.

"Nice," I said. Blackie growled in response. "Relax, I wasn't talking to you."

An hour later, I hear a car pull into the driveway. I peeked out the curtain and saw that the occupants of the trailer had returned.

"Ah, they're here, Blackie."

I stood by the window, facing the front door, and waited for Allison and Rich to enter. I heard the car doors close, them talking, and then their footfalls on the front steps. A key was inserted into the other side of the knob, it turned, and the door opened.

Rich was the first to step over the threshold. His brow creased and a frown formed on his face when he saw me.

"Who the fuck are you?"

I pulled out the gun I'd been carrying.

"What's wrong, hon?" Allison asked and then paused when she saw me before her holding the gun.

"Come in," I said, "both of you."

"Who the fuck are you?" Rich said again.

"Never mind that right now," I growled. "Come in and sit down." I motioned to the couch with the gun.

I saw Allison look over at Blackie, who was growling and tugging at his leash.

"Don't worry, Allison," I said. "He's muzzled, he can't hurt you."

"You know my name?" Allison said.

"Of course I do, I know Rich's name, too, but that's not all I know about you two. Now sit."

Allison sat on the end furthest from Blackie, and Rich practically sat on top of her. They both eyed the pit bull warily.

"What's the matter?" I asked. "I thought you two like dogs like this—mean and viscous. In fact you had one, a gray pit bull here with you last year. I heard he was so endearing."

"How do you know that?" Rich demanded, his eyes never leaving the gun.

"Because," I said. "It got loose on Easter and ate my stepdaughter's dog. That ruined her Easter real fast and she's still haunted by it, my ex-wife, too."

"That's why you're here?" Rich said. "Because of some stupid fucking dog?"

"I hope you're talking about the pit bull," I said, "and not Beau."

"Who's Beau...?" Allison asked, confused.

"That was the name of the dog you two killed."

"Bullshit," Rich said.

"We didn't kill anything," Allison added.

"Oh, but you did," I said to Allison. "You admitted to my ex that the pit bull you had had ate a cat and then went after your niece. That it was taken away but you two dipshits got it back. You knew how dangerous that dog was, yet you chose to have it around. That makes you both responsible. You two are just as guilty, if not more so, than that damn pit bull."

"So what?" Rich said. "You've come here to kill us, to get your revenge?"

"Yeah, Rich, I'm here for revenge," I said. "You caused my ex and step-daughter great pain and that pisses me off; it enrages me. No one hurts my family and gets away with it."

Throughout our conversation, Blackie continued to act up.

"Why do you even care?" Allison asked. "She's your ex-wife and her daughter isn't even yours. They ain't your family no more."

"Just because my marriage didn't last and just because the girl is not mine doesn't mean don't love them or that they're not family. Of course, I wouldn't expect you two pieces of shit to understand that. All you're worried about is your next fix."

"Screw you," Rich hissed.

"You'll never get away with this," Allison breathed.

"Oh, I think I will, Allison," I said. "I think I will."

"How do you plan on doing it?" Rich asked, licking his lips.

"Don't worry about it," I said. "I have it covered."

I stepped into the kitchen, keeping my gun trained in Allison and Rich's general direction. With my free hand, I took the mirror from the kitchen table. I walked over and gave it to Allison.

"Got some in your pocket?" I asked.

Allison nodded.

"Dish out some lines for you and Rich."

Allison looked confused and went to open her mouth.

"Don't question me," I said. "Just do it."

Allison pulled the coke from her front pocket and made four lines on the small mirror.

"Good," I said. "Now you do two, and Rich, you do the other two."

"What the fuck is the point of this?" Rich hissed.

"Don't question me," I repeated. "Just do what I say."

"Fuck you, man!" he yelled but did as he was told.

As they did their lines, I stepped back into the kitchen and pulled a steak knife from the pile of dirty dishes. Its blade and handle were covered in dry, crusted food. I was glad to be wearing gloves. I placed the knife on a small end table sitting against the wall opposite the couch.

"Here's how it is going to work," I said. "When I tell you to, Rich, you're gonna unhook the leash and remove the muzzle from…"

"The hell I am!" Rich yelled.

"You're gonna do it, Rich," I said. "Or so help me I'll shoot Allison right now."

"Go 'head," Rich shrugged. "You're gonna kill us anyway." His eyes were glazed over thanks to the lines.

"Oh, but I never said I was going to kill you, Rich. I only said I was here for revenge. I don't have to kill you to get that." I smiled. "If you noticed, I put a knife on the end table. If Allison can get it and use it before Blackie does too much damage, both of you might live."

"How do we know you won't shoot us afterwards?" Allison asked. She was sweating now and her mouth kept opening and closing as she began to fly away in her mind, the drugs taking hold.

"You don't," I said.

Allison and Rich looked at each other. They spoke without speaking. She nodded, he nodded.

"All right," Rich slurred. "I'll do it."

Rich stood and bent over towards Blackie, who growled and jumped at him, the dog's leash holding the animal at bay.

"When he starts to undo the muzzle, Allison, you go for the knife," I said.

"Yeah, and quick, too," Rich added. "I may be able to hold this fucker back for a few seconds but not any longer than that."

Allison, with her lips pressed firmly together, nodded and moved to the edge of the sofa.

"Here goes nothing," Rich mumbled. He tried to pin Blackie between his shoulder and the couch. He undid the leash, moved his hands up to the muzzle, and yelled, "Get the knife, Allison!"

Despite Blackie's strength and reckless nature, Rich was able to hold him still long enough to get the muzzle off. Once it was off, the pit bull snapped at Rich's face, but Rich jerked his head back and got his hands on the pit bull's head.

Allison snatched up the knife and turned. She raised it as she hurried, tripped over her own feet, and fell into Rich. The hit knocked Rich off balance; he fell forward and his grip on Blackie loosened.

The dog pulled his head free and bit Rich on the neck. Screaming, Rich fell backwards, holding his damaged, bloody throat. Blackie was on him in an instant, tearing at his throat. Allison screamed and righted herself, then retrieved the dirty knife and shoved it in Blackie's side. I swear that I could hear the sound of metal slicing into flesh as the blade bit deep

Blackie yelped, long and loud.

Allison pulled the knife free and plunged deeply into the animal's side again. Blackie yelped once more and turned his attention to Allison, blood now coating his dark muzzle. It dripped on the dirty floor in a steady staccato.

Rich lay on his back, blood bubbling up out of his ravaged throat, his eyes bulging from their sockets.

Allison screamed when Blackie lunged at her, but her grip on the knife was solid and it pierced the dog's chest as she fell back with the animal on top of her. She pulled the knife free and planted it in his chest again, blood spraying from the blade to paint the walls scarlet.

Blackie looked like a demon from Hell. He yelped every time the knife bit him but other than that, and the blood, the wounds didn't seem to bother him. Allison tried to squirm her way out from under Blackie but couldn't. She twisted the knife and screamed as the dog sank his teeth into her neck. Her screams didn't last long.

Things hadn't gone exactly as planned, and I panicked as the dog began to tear into Allison. I rushed out of the living room, through the kitchen, and out the back door before Blackie could turn his attention towards me. He was bleeding pretty good but still had some fight in him.

I went behind the trailer and hunched down, hidden in the bushes. Fifteen minutes passed before I regained my composure enough to get up. I went back around to the back door and cracked it open, keeping my shoulder and weight against it just in case.

"Blackie?" I called. "Here boy."

Instead of claws on the linoleum and viscous growls running at me, I heard whining coming from within. Blackie sounded hurt, like he was dying, but I had to make sure. He was too dangerous to be allowed to live anyway.

I pulled the door open the rest of the way and stepped inside. I peeked around the corner to the living room and saw Blackie lying next to Rich and Allison. The dog was the only one still breathing, and judging by how shallow his breaths were, he wouldn't be doing so for much longer.

I stepped back out of the trailer and walked to my truck. I had no regrets on what I'd done, though I really hadn't planned on killing them. Allison and Rich were trash, and if left to their own devices, would no doubt overdose and die one of these days anyway.

They just went to Hell sooner instead of later.

As I got into my truck and drove off, I knew I could tell Brianna that she was safe, that Death wouldn't be coming anytime soon to claim her.

The Grim Reaper had already gotten his fill today.

GRAINS OF BONE-WHITE SAND

PETE CLARK

Sunlight dapples my eyelids. My eyes ache more than ever now, and with each new dawn I wake with dread. It is cold too, this morning.

A thin layer of frost glues the edge of my coat to the pavement, spikes my hair into messy peaks. I run a hand through it, and hear, in the dead quiet of morning, soft crackles as the spikes dissolve. My nose is icy; my cheeks feel red and chapped. I sit up slowly, aware of pains that are too numerous to single out.

The cold smoothness of the glass behind me is running with rivulets of freezing condensation, but it prevents me from falling.

As I stretch my legs out, hearing the pops and cracks of my stiff joints, I see that the gloves I'm wearing are tattered, both thumbs poking rudely through. I smell terrible, I am sure, but I have long since lost the ability to judge my own odor.

I draw up my legs and hug them close to me. The city is still asleep at this hour, and I revel in the quiet. The sun begins to rise, and I imagine that it rises just for me. It's beautiful. I can never forget the desperation of my situation, but I've learned to push it away, hide it in some cloistered corner of my brain, where I daren't yet mine.

My thoughts turn slowly, inevitably, to breakfast. I smile. I have a nice smile, and I'm lucky that I still have all my teeth, that my skin is clear and smooth, and that my hair is not too unkempt.

I'm lucky that people still find in them some measure of pity, and I need that. I don't eat all that often. You have to learn to live on very little, sometimes nothing. I read of a man who survived for over four months on water alone. I try not to better that.

I stand and stretch. The sun this morning is truly wonderful. There are long, gray morning shadows, and where there is land, there are small patches of glistening white frost. Everywhere else, it melts quickly.

The street lamps flickered out two hours ago, and such is the time of year that they will be flickering back to life in eight or nine hours. My feet are still cold, and I shift them into the sun, stamping lightly. I'm not happy, and yet something keeps waking me in the mornings, keeps me going through the motions of day after day. It's the same thing that has kept me going for nearly thirteen years. I'm not sure what that something is, but I'm sure I will know it when I see it. It's waiting for me.

I'm standing on a pavement running the length of a quiet city street. My hair is long, my beard thick but relatively un-matted, for I comb it and my hair regularly.

I'm wearing ratty shoes that have lasted me for ten years or more, and here and there they are held together with strips of plastic bag and parcel tape. Of my three pairs of trousers, I'm wearing my worst. The other two are folded into the bag I use as a pillow. Also in the bag are several t-shirts. Over all this I'm wearing a dark green Army jacket that I found. It's lined with fake fur, although I'm sure it was never Army issue. Most of it is hanging torn and shredded like giant cobwebs.

I look up and down the street. There are few awake, one or two early-rising shopkeepers. I see one now, scurrying like an over-sized ant to and from his shop, arms laden with fruit boxes. My mouth begins to salivate. I walk towards the shopkeeper, and as they almost all do, he keeps his head down, content to know of my existence but ignore it.

I kick a soft drink can down the road in front of me, and it isn't until I hear the muted rattle of its passage, that I fully realize the depth of the silence. My breath makes soft white plumes in the air, and I walk through them. The open shop is very close now. The shopkeeper looks up and sees me coming, then looks quickly away. I think it's possibly because my eyes resemble those of a wild animal, a wolf perhaps. I stuff my hands deep into the pockets of my jacket.

The shopkeeper mumbles something incoherent, and I try to be friendly. I nod my head and mumble back. No words, just cautious sounds. I see his arm move suddenly, in a blur, and realize he's thrown something at me. Or rather, *to* me. My hand snatches the projectile from the air with scarcely a thought, and I break into a wide, toothy grin as I feel the cold crisp hardness of an apple in my palm. It's as big as a baseball, red and shiny as fresh blood. I thank him with real words this time and laugh.

I bite into the apple, and it is lush and sweet. The juice runs into my beard, but I ignore the stickiness for now. For a moment I can forget where and who I am and enjoy my breakfast.

But it's over too soon and I throw the core and pips into a trashcan. My hands thread their way back into my jacket pockets, for although it is slightly warmer in the sun, there is still a bitter wind curling its fingers around me.

There is a bit more life to the city now. My watch has been broken for four years, but I can guess the time pretty accurately. It is around seven-thirty.

I see my first car of the morning. Its exhaust belches oily-blue smoke, and I watch the plumes twist and cavort in the cold air, thin tendrils reaching after the car like dead hands. I cough deeply, not liking the deep rattle that follows each hacking cough, or the moisture welling in my eyes. The apple has left tiny slivers of skin between my teeth, and I find a park bench and spend a few happy moments picking them out.

The street meets with the main road here, and at all four corners of the junction I can see the city open herself up to me. It spreads as far as I can see. I stretch my legs and drop one on top of the other. For a while, I'm content. The sun warms my face and I turn to it, closing my eyes.

The city is truly a magnificent place, and here is its true beauty. Here at its heart. Cars appear from nowhere, roaring past, their numbers increasing into a flowing metal stream, the faces of the drivers merging, becoming one face, parts of it content, parts irate, parts distant, as if the people have far more worry on their minds than they outwardly show. I watch them pass.

The last piece of apple comes loose and I grind it between my teeth with childish satisfaction. I have been here long enough to nod off, I think. It's perhaps nine o'clock, probably a little before. The air is humming with life. People traveling to work, to the stores. Ah, for those luxuries. I used to work; only now I can't remember where.

A woman sits down next to me. At least, she's on the same bench as me, but is sitting as far away as she can manage, stuffing herself into the corner and studying her fingernails as though they were priceless jewels. I turn to look at her and my heart stutters. I know this woman!

I can't place her name, but I know I was married once. Jean, or Jane. Is this her? I look again and she looks back. I see her face full on. It's not my wife. My heart is beating fast and I grin stupidly. I'm sure I appear a madman to her, grinning through a thick swatch of dirty beard. She moves hastily on, as the world does. Her perfume does not share her haste, and hangs lazily in the air. It tickles my nostrils and I fight with a sneeze. It wins.

I stand and turn to meet the nestling of storefronts before me. Which way? I choose straight on because it seems less effort that way. As I walk, I find I'm thinking of the woman. Who is she? I ask myself out loud.

A young couple shoot quizzical looks my way but I ignore them. I must seem no different to the hundreds of babbling tramps that wander the city.

My eyes are open but shock flares them wider. My heart races. I think I'm wetting myself. A noise, blaring louder and louder until it threatens to split my ear drums, is drilling its way into my head. I can't place the noise, but suddenly something snaps and it's clear to me.

A car horn. I turn to my right and see the car, its grille, like bared teeth, inches from my leg. In the air is the bitter sting of burning rubber. The angry driver is yelling, but the volume of the horn has temporarily deafened me, and I can't make out the words.

I have walked blindly out into the road. Before waiting for me to move, the driver wrenches his car around me, an angry squeal of tires.

I trot quickly to the other side of the road, and rest my weight on a lamppost, breathing heavily. My heart bumps and jitters under my ribs and my legs quiver as if they are about to drop me to the ground.

I feel coldness as the air hits the wet patch at my crotch. As I calm, the reality of what happens hits me suddenly. Was I really that close to death? I begin to cry as the relief washes over me. On the tails of relief follow shame and desperation. Would anyone care if I had died? I mean, *really* care? Still hitching breath, I manage to hobble away past more storefronts.

As I walk, a thought hits me so violently that I stagger into the street.

What if I had been killed back there? What if the driver hadn't seen me, hadn't stopped? Would it be better if I were dead? I list everything I would miss, but the truth of it is I would miss very little. I force the thought away. My knees have stopped their ragged shaking, my heart beats normally.

My chest feels abused, raw, but I manage to draw breath. Sleep comes easily when you're homeless, and comes easiest of all when your belly is empty and your body is drained of nutrients and vigor.

I find a large tree, this one still frosted from the cold, and I wrestle myself into the confines of its buttresses. My bag serves me again as a pillow and I wrap the tattered remains of my coat around my legs, which I have curled under me.

My dreams are horrid; scaly things invading and tormenting me. I dream of cars, of great shining grilles with teeth that threaten to unravel me.

I dream of death and I dream of a man. He has become a friend to me, in past months, yet I never see his face. I twist and contort myself in sleep, but no one cares.

I'm left to my nightmare.

I'm standing in sand up to my ankles...it's cold and bites into me as if every grain was gifted with bristling needle teeth...wind whips around me but I have no coat...nothing to warm my freezing skin...as I look down at myself I see I'm completely naked...my skin is peaked infinitely with goosebumps...blue with the cold...

There is nothing to see...the dreamscape is as desolate as I always feared it would be...dunes upon dunes of billowing sand white as if sun bleached...but there is no sun...the wind drops but the cold remains as if it is within me...I start to walk forward, but there is no front or back here...north is as south is as east is as west...up is as down...I appear as white as the biting sand...motionless...emotionless...a man is walking towards me now out of the distance...he has always been there...waiting...my dream-self...

It's the friend I have had in every dream I can remember...I'm jealous of his dark robes that drape across his wide shoulders...of the cowl that protects his face from the sand...the sand...always the biting sand...

I know that if I were to remove that cowl he would appear as I do...my twin...I laugh...he echoes the sound...his laugh is dead...flat...cold...coming across the wastes of sand...I raise my hands and he copies…I'm drugged…my limbs heavy…I fight it…and it is winning…

The man beckons and I walk towards him…passing oceans of bleached sand…still the man remains distant…always the same number of footfalls away from me…he's walking away as I walk towards…and yet we are facing each other…

He stops…tilts his head…I tilt mine and I wonder who is leading who…am I him? Is he me? My nakedness is covered now by a robe like his and we could be as one…I draw back the hood of the robe hoping he will do the same…

As I watch, the man finally draws the cowl from his own head and I recoil…unable to stop myself…it is plainly me I'm looking at…the same awkward tilt to my mouth…the same deep set eyes…the same wide cheekbones and high forehead…and where my own face is bristling with beard…his is clean…no hair on it whatsoever…I see the reason suddenly…he is burned…this version of me…horribly burned so that his face appears nothing more than a pasty mass of scar tissue…I could be looking at death itself…and then it smiles at me…the scars bunching and stretching horribly around the mouth and eyes…I scream…

My own face wrinkles in sympathy and I feel I could reach right to him and pull the mask off…if I were to do so I would see myself underneath…I reach towards this hideous parody…expecting it to retreat but it doesn't…expecting myself to finally wake but I don't…

Suddenly I'm next to it…a reverse mirror image of it…of me…breathing the reek from it…from the glistening maw that is its face…its eyes have gone…it no longer looks human…like me…its arms are wizened claws…and they clutch at me so violently I'm thrown off my feet…my lungs seize and breath is expelled in one long desperate gasp…

It reaches again for me…its wizened arms reaching higher and higher until it grasps my throat tightly…I gasp as it pushes my head down…I present the crown of my head to it…wait for the killing stroke…it doesn't come…

It takes my skull...strangely soft...into its putrid maw...it melds to the contours of the thing's palate...my chin is resting on its tongue and I can hear the boiling acid in its stomach... I vomit at the stench of it...I can see down the throat...down the esophagus that is a wasted tube of dead flesh...

The pressure from its grasping hands relaxes considerably but I do not try to pull my head from its jaws...I feel a profound loss every time I move so I remain still...push my head further in...blind now to the sights and smells of it...and it begins to feel warm and soft...sensual almost...I'm an infant now...the baby is crying and I know that it is crying not through fear or hunger but rather because everything it has ever known...the womb...the warmth...has been wrenched from it cruelly...because it knows that all it will experience now is pain...dirt...excretion...hurt...

I hear a deep laugh beginning in the creature's gut...my laugh of course...as I realize who it is...who I am...

Death...

And now this feeling I have as I kiss the insides of the creature's mouth...rub my face into the soft tongue...caress the fleshy softness... I recognize it as the feeling of being born back to the womb...back to the sensual protective darkness that begins life and inevitably...must end it...

I reach my hands up and the jaws open wider to accommodate me... I start to clamber frantically inside...using my legs to push deeper...it seems impossibly big as I begin to disappear into the putrid blackness...suddenly the mouth shuts behind me and I'm left in pitch blackness...I yell...hawking great lungfuls of stinking air to fuel my cries...

As a great snaking umbilical cord wraps itself around me and I writhe against its greasy pulsing length...suddenly it grows tight and pulls me in...the mouth starts to tip me forwards...I know it means to swallow me and I feel tingling anticipation...it means to end my life...or begin my death...it is the same...

I reach into the throat meaning to pull myself further in...I encounter rows of viciously serrated teeth... I pull my hands away from the pain and find them hopelessly ruined and torn...a violent tipping of the tongue and I'm gone...deep...deep into the cave of its throat...deep into myself...for we are one and the same...the teeth rake at me...I'm a fetus...curled and defenseless...I smell the pit of its stomach...feel splashes of the acid on my face and arms...before I die I hear the laughter again...then...nothing...

Then I'm awake and it's afternoon. The sun is sinking already so I know it must be at least four thirty.

I stink of piss. I must have vomited in my sleep. I see there is blood in the mess beside me.

I feel strange. Never in my thirteen years as a vagabond have I felt such peace. I feel terribly warm, yet I can see from the hats and scarves, and from the frosty plumes of breath around me, that it's cold.

As I stand and stretch, I realize suddenly what it is I have been searching for these years. It pops into my head as sharply and audibly as a snapping twig.

I'm looking for Death.

Quite simply. I have lived this life of misery for too long and I'm sick of it. Sick of the hunger, the cold, the thirst. Sick of the danger, the withering stares and the illness that are constant bed fellows. I'm lonely and desolate, all I have or once had is gone, extinguished like a fragile flame. I have the answer now. Death awaits me, reaching to me with arms that promise peace and calm and happiness.

It's so simple. I shrug off my coat and stand in the chill of the winter evening. I feel no cold. I laugh and laugh.

As I walk from my bed, I slip my arms into my jacket, preferring the ease of wearing it to the clumsiness of carrying it. The air has become cold, and I can almost taste the thinness of it.

The idea of dying doesn't fill me with the cold dread it once did. Instead, I feel a longing for the peace that has evaded me for as long as I can remember.

The grass crunches under my feet. The frost has returned, and I prepare for a cold night. I begin to think of food; begin to return to the routine of finding food, eating food and finding shelter.

I then realize I have other plans ahead, and that finding food and shelter need not figure in them. The man in my dreams surfaces in my mind again, shrouded and darkened behind his cowl. I long for his final touch.

I find another tree and lie beneath it. I have vague memories of trying to kill myself once. Seven years ago. Perhaps I knew then what I know now? What I *desire* now? Perhaps not. Stolen headache tablets, spread in a pile like a tiny snow-capped mountain. I remember the sound they made as they tumbled and clattered against one another. Swallowed slowly, one by one, washed down with a half bottle of vodka. My hands were steady, and my heart a peaceful rhythm.

It comforted me as I prepared for my death. How many heartbeats left? Three hundred? A thousand? Ten? Nothing seemed to happen for a long time. I dozed and woke with metronomic regularity, and then...

There was light suddenly all around me, and pain stabbed my gut like a knife. My face contorted with agony, eyes flared and mouth frothed like a horse in the throes of madness. The brightness changed. Occasional flashes of color, too bright for me to register. My head seemed to lift from my shoulders and there was a roiling in my gut.

Vomit spewed across my legs. Black in the moonlight, presumably with blood. Still my head rose and I felt I could turn to look down at my thrashing, spasming body below me. My stomach rose and fell rapidly, and with each new contortion, a fresh gobbet of vomit spattered me.

My head sank suddenly without warning and by degrees the contortions slowed and stopped. Sudden blackness. I fell to my jacket and let death take me.

Yet I woke and lived.

The memory is now too much for my fragile mind. I'm sick, violently, and I fall into blackness again.

I become aware of the warmth of the sun on my face as I wake. I realize with some dismay that I'm still alive. I'm hollowed out, like a shell, my innards wrenched from their moorings like so much crab meat.

I stare at the splatter of vomit across my legs and see undigested apple littering the dark redness like stars in a dusky sky. Tears wet my cheeks as I try to stand and fall back, weakened.

Death won't come for me. I know that now. I will have to find him myself. Urgency lifts me. I must do this. I realize I am chanting this mantra.

I must do this.

I must find Death.

The city is alien, and suddenly it feels like death is everywhere. I feel like a tourist— death's tourist—among the throng. All seems strange to me, as if I hadn't looked at it every day of my life for thirteen years or more.

My head feels crushed and my neck and stomach muscles feel stretched, violated. I'm cold without my coat. I stagger across ever busy streets, mindless to the traffic, the screeching tires, wailing horns. I walk through crowds of people that aren't there.

Dark roads lead off the main street and the perspective of the houses that line them draws me into their darkness, like a wooded path in a fairy tale. I take the furthest one from the bustle of the city.

Front yards and pavements are littered with the corpses of deceased bicycles, shopping carts and old shoes. Windows in the houses nearest the entrance to the road are clean and sparkle in the sun. Further in they are either smashed or boarded over like wounds. I encounter few people and those that I do avert their eyes. Soon enough I stop looking at them and walk. Hunger gnaws at me pointlessly.

At the last house on the road, facing me before a broken fence and miles of increasing dark, the door hangs limply open. A mattress juts like a tongue, and the windows are half-lidded with yellowing curtains. As if I have been led here, my heart quickens as I walk up the path and enter the house, the first I have been in since leaving my own so many years ago.

The stench of the place hits me like a slap, and I reel, noticing as I do the discarded needles like a glassy snow drift in one corner. I walk in a fugue through to what I presume is a sitting room and I'm struck from behind.

Pain flares suddenly, violently in my head, ringing at my temple. My legs collapse and I'm dead weight on the carpet.

When I look up, a man is standing over me, a torrent of words escaping him, or so I imagine. I seem to have gone deaf, the blow blurring my senses.

The pain fades as the man hits me again. I have time to study his face, pocked and drawn, a cheese-white blot with hollow eyes like burns. I see a flash of metal. The man berates me further, although I'm still deaf to his ranting. I try to tell him I have no need for his drugs but he hits me again, and follows that with a flurry of kicks, surprisingly solid despite his apparent frailty. The metal flashes again and I have time to register a blade.

Just barely.

Heat blooms in my chest and when I look down, I see I'm skewered. Blood oozes slowly around the handle and coats the blade. I laugh. The man withdraws the knife, and I recognize and appreciate the look of horror on his face. Can I thank him? If only he knew. I try, between giggles. Everything blurs again and the pain seems unable to creep through the fog. My laughter further enrages him and he stabs me again.

More pain fills me as the blade slips delicately between my ribs into my heart. A sickening release and blood courses from the wound. Grayness edges across my vision, and my last true sight is of the man turning, dropping the knife. I watch the blood slip from its gleam as it lets go its hold on my fluids.

Blackness. There is the sound of my heart beating its last and then there is nothing. No sound, no sight, no feeling. It is as if I have ceased to exist, except that I am somehow aware of this fact.

I suffer a moment or two of this nothingness and then feel cold biting wind and hear the rustle that I know is the sound of grains of sand knocking and jostling over one another.

I'm standing in sand up to my ankles...it bites me as if every grain was gifted with bristling needle teeth...in front of me is... my twin...its jaws drops wide and I begin my climb into the maw once again...the smells and sounds of death affront me...and to accent them is the throb where the drug addict's knife ended me...

I lay my head on the glossy tongue...stroke my arms wide across it...it becomes as a second coupling with a new lover...no less exciting...anticipative...but less anxious and fearful...familiar... I rub my face and torso into the floor of this cavern... I curl like the fetus I'm becoming and begin sucking on my thumb... I almost cry out as I feel the greasy umbilical cord join me to the twin who swallows me...

A pulsating movement underneath and the floor of the cave softens further...blackness begins to drop from the fleshy walls as the mouth decays around me... I sink a way into the tongue as it rots...it starts to tip me down the throat and the teeth begin their work anew...tearing me and pulling me in...

I cry out and attempt to withdraw...my arms are caught and are shredding...pain washes like fire and I scream... I manage to release myself somehow... I'm free for seconds until my legs are snagged on the grasping teeth that seem to have life...my legs are stripped of skin and then of flesh as they are pulled further in...

I scream again and beg for it to stop...but of course it doesn't...not when my chest is punctured...not when the teeth reach my neck and tear at the skin there...it doesn't stop when the umbilical tears loose...sending viscera spilling hotly down the rotting tube of its throat...

And when the pain seems to have reached its peak...it doubles and triples and magnifies by multiples of thousands as my skull is crushed by the peristalsis within the rotting tube of its throat...my brain presses against the bone briefly before being forced out through nose and mouth and ears... I moan...no longer able to scream...how can I still be aware? I beg again for it to stop...and still it doesn't...

It swallows...finally...and I boil in its acids...a fleshy pulp and still unmercifully aware to the end of my pain and plight... I have no form...only feeling...and so am forced to experience my own dissolution...digestion...excretion...this last fills me with such anguish that I scream...and scream...and scream...silently...

Once out of the creature my soul turns and watches as the creature slinks away...no longer pretending human form...I can make no sense of it...

I hang in the air over a pile of this creature's excrement...in the mess are clearly definable shapes...a femur here...ribs there...caging a domed segment of my skull...as I watch the wind picks up and the feces starts to

crumble...already drying...the bones crumble with it...crumble into
dust...into...

Into...

Into...

Suddenly it hits me...

My death is nothing. No pleasures. No sensuality. It's not the comforting womb that I believed it to be. It's simply a cold, biting desert. My bones have vanished.

I make the connection. I realize that if I had a heart, and it hadn't already been pierced, surely it would burst.

The creature has betrayed me. This desert *is* death.

It's nothing more or less than the powdered bones of billions of tricked souls just like me.

He has shit them all out to rot and crumble among the bone-white sand. Bone-white because it *is* bone. And here I am, too. I fear I will never be unaware. Mercy will not visit me. Or rather, us.

I can hear so many others crying with me.

I'm no different now.

My death is a grain of sand in a desert.

My crying joins the cacophony and it is a horrible sound.

RAW MEAT

DAN LOUBIER

I recognized the smell as soon as I opened the door. An odor very similar to that of raw meat filled my nose. Not rotted or decaying meat; just raw.

You know, like when you first open a butcher-wrapped package of ground beef? Maybe not the worst smell in the world, but certainly not the most pleasant either. Anyway, *that* aroma filled my nose as soon as I walked into my apartment building.

A minute earlier, when I'd pulled into the driveway that separates the two main buildings, I saw several police cars, as well as a white van with the words, **Fairfield County Coroner** written across the back doors, parked along the side closest to my building.

Holy shit! Somebody died! I wondered.

Trying not to stare out the passenger window, I acted casual, so as not to draw any attention to myself, as I drove past the vehicles and toward the parking lot. I hadn't done anything wrong, but as a rule, I generally don't enjoy police activity in my building so, as curious as I was to their presence, I definitely didn't want to give them any reason to talk to me. Especially since I'd had a few beers in me already—didn't need them sticking a breathalyzer down my throat, and especially since someone was dead in there.

After I'd parked and reached my building, I kept my head down as I pulled the door closed behind me. When I turned toward the hallway, I shifted my gaze upward, only slightly, but enough to see an officer standing half-inside the doorway to one of the apartments.

Shit, I thought. *I gotta walk by this guy now. Great.*

I stuffed my hands into the pockets of my hoodie—I'd spilled alcohol more than once tonight and didn't want the officer to catch a whiff—and proceeded to walk down the hall. Casually. Nonchalant. Carefree. Maybe just a little too carefree.

"Excuse me, sir, can I ask you a few questions?"

Damn it. Of course he would ask *me* a few questions. I was walking right by after all. It probably made his job easier, just grabbing us as we come in. God forbid he would have to go door-to-door in a three-floor apartment building. God forbid he actually did his job. God forbid he...

"Uh, yeah, sure," I said.

He was young, definitely new to the force. I could tell he was new because he was about the same age as me—just-out-of-college age. His dark hair was shaped into a crew-cut, which was almost a very short flat-top—a dead give-away that he was a newbie. He was also built like a goddamn half-back. Another sign he was new because, in my experience, older cops are either overweight or out-of-shape, or both. It's pretty much the new ones who come in clean-shaven, short-haired, buffed up. They're the ones trying to impress their veteran peers.

He held a clipboard in his hands. I could see a list of names typed out. I recognized a lot of them. They were people who lived in the building. I guessed he'd already started making the rounds because several names had checkmarks next to them, while others were left unchecked.

Well, kudos to you, I thought. Maybe the young buck is a go-getter after all.

"Do you live here in the building?" Flat-top asked. He wore a gruff expression on his face, which I could tell was forced—yet another sign of a newbie. It even seemed like his voice was a bit unnatural, as if he'd made a conscious attempt to lower his tone.

Real tough guy, I thought.

"Yeah," I said.

"Which apartment?"

I removed a hand from my hoodie and extended it down the hall. "One-oh-four. Down on the end."

Shit, why did I take my hand out!

"And what's your full name, sir?"

"Bryan Bishop," I answered.

He looked down at his clipboard and put a check next to my name. When he looked back at me, he narrowed his eyebrows—a failed attempt at intimidation. I clenched my teeth and tried not to laugh.

"Were you here earlier tonight, Mr. Bishop?" he asked.

I looked up at the ceiling and let out a long exhale, a visible showing of my attempt to remember the last several hours. Then I met his eyes again.

"I left around six tonight. I'm just getting back now. Why, did something happen?"

"Where did you go?" Flat-top asked, completely dismissing my question.

"McDougal's Tavern," I said, and then immediately regretted it.

"Have you been drinking?"

Oh well, no sense in lying to him. "Yeah, I met up with some friends and had a few while we were watching the UConn game."

"And your friends can confirm this?"

"Yup."

"Who won the game?"

"UCONN!" I bellowed out, thrusting a closed fist above my head. He wasn't impressed with my demeanor, but I could tell he was at least somewhat satisfied with my answers.

He stayed quiet for the moment, his eyes down, as he scribbled information onto the sheet attached to the clipboard. Meanwhile, I looked around to see what else was going on. None of the other units had their doors open, just the one in front of which I currently stood. That's when I noticed something out of the corner of my eye: flashes of light and movement to the left.

Movement inside the open door of unit 107. I casually glanced inside the apartment. All the lights were on. Officers were walking back and forth, pointing out items or areas of interest. There was a woman holding a camera. She was taking pictures of something on the floor. As the camera flash went off again, she moved and I could see what it was. The owner of unit 107 lay dead on the floor—his head was missing.

I turned and vomited against the wall in the hallway. I doubled over as the Miller Lite started ejecting itself back out of my system.

"Mr. Bishop, are you all right?" Flat-top asked.

I put a hand up when I sensed him coming closer.

"It's okay," I said, between heaves. "I've never seen a…" I threw up again.

"I'm sorry you had to see that." To my surprise, his apology actually sounded genuine. "We had the door closed earlier, but officers have been in and out all night, and the neighbors haven't been nosey at all so it was just easier to leave it open." Another officer walked out the door, between us, just as Flat-top finished his sentence.

I put a hand against the wall and rested there for a moment.

Damn, not my new Clarks, I thought as I stood there, bent over, staring down at the vomit on my shoes.

"What happened to him?" I asked. I wiped my hand across my mouth to remove any residual vomit, then I rubbed it against my pant leg.

I could tell he was hesitant to give me any details by the way he looked around. When he stopped checking to see who might be within earshot, he turned to me.

"We're not real certain on the details at this point," he said, lowering his voice. "But we know that Mr. Daneyhill was attacked and murdered inside his apartment tonight."

"Holy shit!" I gasped.

"Yeah, it's pretty gruesome in there. We should probably keep the door closed." He reached over and grabbed the handle and closed the door.

"Do you think it was someone in the building?" I asked.

"Unfortunately, I can't say. But we're looking into all possibilities. As of right now, it doesn't look like there was any forced entry into the victim's unit, so we think he probably knew his attacker, .and that person might live here in the building."

"Jesus Christ!" I said. "Well, shouldn't you guys evacuate this place or something? Take everyone to the station for questioning?"

"We're trying to get an idea of who was in the building at the time of the murder. Once we do that, we'll have a good idea of who we're looking at, if in fact the suspect resides here."

"Do you *have* a suspect?" I asked.

He took the clipboard with one hand and folded his arms over his chest. His expression suddenly became cold. I had probably asked too much.

"I can't say anything more at this time."

Yep. I definitely asked too much. His voice had returned to that forced, almost robotic, tone as when he first spoke to me.

At this point, the officer who had come through the door a few minutes ago returned. He stepped between us again and opened the door to Daneyhill's apartment, but as he stepped inside, he stopped, held the door open with his foot, and turned back to Officer Flat-top. He then leaned in close and proceeded to whisper something to him.

As he did this, I straightened up and peeked inside Daneyhill's apartment again. I was able to get another glimpse of the horror inside. Massive amounts of blood spatter on the walls and on the floor. Daneyhill's left arm lay at his side, the hand palm up. His lower half was out of my view, behind a row of floor cabinets. His right hand and arm were eclipsed by the rest of his lifeless torso.

Where his head *used* to be, there was only the shredded, fleshy remains of his neck. I tried not to stare but I couldn't help it. His head was completely severed. Gone. Nowhere to be seen. It wasn't anywhere in the apartment, at least not in my field of vision. And as I stared at the man's neck, at the way the flesh lay torn, the way his blood had spilled out on the floor, all I could think of was the way warm lasagna collapses back into the pan after the first piece has been cut out.

"Mr. Bishop?"

"Huh?" I said, half-panicked that I'd seen something I shouldn't have.

"I think that's all the questions I have for you right now," Flat-top said. The other officer was already gone. He must have slipped back inside while I was gawking at Daneyhill's remains. "Are you going to be home for the rest of the night?"

"Uh, yeah. Yes, of course."

"Okay. Well, I appreciate your cooperation, Mr. Bishop. There's going to be quite a police presence through the night, so the building is safe."

"Thank you, Officer. If there's anything else, I'm in…"

"One-oh-four. I know. Have a good night."

He was done with me. He'd probably been assigned to some new task by the officer who'd been whispering to him. Without another word, I nodded my head and walked past him toward my apartment.

As I walked, I thought of pulling out my phone and texting my friends what had happened, but that might have drawn some unwanted attention so I decided against it.

Daneyhill's dead! Murdered!

I still couldn't believe it.

He was fucking BEHEADED! I thought.

That part was really messing me up. I wondered what kind of blade one would need to cut off a person's head. I thought about the strength it would have required to cut through the muscle, tendons, bone…it was all surreal. Fucking Daneyhill, man. Who'd had it out for him? The officer said it might have been someone Daneyhill knew, someone who lived in the building. That was just disturbing. I've been here two years and I knew most of the people who live in the thirty units in my building, but I'd never figured any of them to go ape-shit crazy like that. Who the hell would do such a thing?

As I got to my door, I reached into my pocket for my keys. I turned back to look down the hall, back toward Daneyhill's place. Officer Flat-top was gone. The *real* detectives were probably inside, performing the actual investigation. They'd probably stuck the new guy outside the main door to catch people as they came into the building. Strange that he would leave now though.

I shrugged it off, stuck my key into the door handle and turned.

My apartment was dark. The light that spilled in from the main hallway lit up only the entrance to my condo, but I could see the small side table that stood against the wall in the entryway. Objects that were farther away were rendered as silhouettes. I normally left a light on in the living room on nights I went out, but for some reason, I didn't leave one on this time. Then again, it was probably still light out when I left. Who turns on lights when it's not dark out yet?

I stepped into my apartment and closed the door, then dropped my keys on the side table and kicked off my shoes as I walked down the small front hallway and into the living room. My head was still spinning and I was ready to crash on the couch and watch some TV.

As I reached the end of the hall, I immediately turned left, into my darkened kitchen. Moonlight shone in from the window above the sink. Several of my appliances cast elongated shadows against the counters, walls and floor. I still couldn't get my head around what had happened to Daneyhill or why. I needed some liquid nerve-calmer before I settled into the cushions of the couch. I pulled open the refrigerator door…and saw something that shocked me to the core.

"Holy shit!" I yelled and slammed the door closed, then fell against a cabinet across from the fridge and slid to the floor. My voice rang in my ears, along with the clinking of glass bottles and containers that fell into each other inside the fridge. I'd slammed the door so hard that I felt the vibration through the floor.

What the hell was that? Did I really just see that?

My head and neck immediately began to feel hot, my pulse throbbing harder and harder. My mind began working surprisingly fast, trying to resolve what I'd just seen.

That's impossible. There's no way I just saw that. There's no way that could be there.

As I sat there on the floor, my mind wandered. I thought about what someone might think if they'd been walking by my kitchen window at that very moment and happened to look in. Would they think I was hurt? Would they think I was *dead*? Would they knock on my door to see if I was okay? Or would they even see me at all? Would I see them?

When I finally got my breathing under control and my thoughts arranged, I slowly stood up. I wiped my sweaty hands on my jeans and took a tentative step toward the fridge. I didn't want to open it.

Stop being a pussy. You didn't see anything. Your mind's just playing tricks.

I stopped thinking for a moment and cleared my head. Reaching out with a trembling hand, it closed around the handle. After another deep breath, I pulled.

At first, I pulled slowly. A sliver of light from inside the fridge spilled out onto the kitchen floor, overlapping the moonlight that cascaded through the window.

I opened the door a little more.

The path of interior light grew larger, wider. I could now see a few items in the fridge: ketchup, orange juice, an unwrapped Snickers bar.

I opened the door a little more.

That's when I noticed the red, viscous fluid pooled up on the middle shelf. It gathered around the milk carton, around the package of cream cheese and a container of grapes.

Oh God, no.

I pulled the door open wide and knew for a fact that my eyes had surely not tricked me. In fact, it was the pair of eyes that stared back at me that left me feeling tricked.

Damn you.

It had been years since anything had happened. I was sure I was cured. Not that I saw a psychiatrist or anything, I'd just assumed I'd outgrown it. Similar to the way people outgrow child-like tendencies. Except this was not the work of a child. This was the work of a monster.

Daneyhill's eyes, milky and lifeless, stared at me from the shelf in the fridge. The head had been wedged between the middle and top shelves in a way that left the jaw pinned shut, but the eyes remained open. It occurred to me then that I was likely staring at the final expression made on the face before death.

No, this is impossible. I've been out all night with…with… Well, I'm drunk and who cares if I can't remember who was there. I know UConn won tonight, so there's that. They played… Temple? Syracuse? Shit, come on, man, you know this, you were there! All right, all right, that's fine. So I can't remember who they played, but I know I left at six. Mike picked me up. Wait! No, no… I drove! I dropped Mike off at home. No wait, he stayed at the bar. Shit – Mike didn't even come out tonight!

And so went my thought process, dozens of false scenarios and delusions of my whereabouts. None of it had actually happened. Sure, I'd gone to a bar, but it wasn't to watch a basketball game.

Then finally, I came to the realization of what *had* happened that night.

I'd left the apartment building at the same time Daneyhill had pulled into the parking lot. I was headed out to the bar to watch the UConn game with some friends. Then I got pissed off when I saw Daneyhill bang his door into my car.

That's when I approached him about it, right there in the parking lot. From twenty yards away I could see the huge dent he'd left on my driver's side door. So I told him, "I'd appreciate it if you could be a little more careful when you park next to my car." You know what he said? That smug asshole told me I shouldn't have parked so close to the line. Then he just walked away from me! Like I should be the one to apologize! Fuck him! I'll show him parking on the line!

So I followed him into the building and to his apartment. He said he was done with me and my bullshit and told me to have a nice night. *My bullshit?* The fat fucker even smiled at me with those squinty, little eyes when he said, "Have a nice night."

So I stuck my foot inside his apartment door, just enough so that the door couldn't close then I pushed my way inside. He told me to get out so I punched him in the jugular. That shut him up. His eyes went really wide and he reached his hands to his throat. Then he started to make this noise that was part-gurgle, part-choke. I told him I was sorry and that I was out of line. I told him to drop his hands and that I would help him out. So he let go of his neck and I grabbed a carving knife off the kitchen counter and went Manson on him.

When I was done, I left his body to lie on the carpet while I looked for a bag to put the head in. Now, I have never understood why that part of me does these things. I guess the other me is a fan of trophies. Anyway, I found some plastic grocery bags in the closet and used one of them.

Then I went back to my apartment and put Daneyhill's head in the fridge. I knew I'd come back home later on, having no memory of what had happened, and probably have a coronary after seeing the fat fuck's eyes staring back at me when I went to get something from the fridge. Some joke.

After that I left the building again. I drove out of the parking lot, having no idea what I was doing or where I was going. I decided to stop at the carwash just in case there was any evidence of my interaction with Daneyhill on my car. Plus, my vehicle was filthy. I stopped at one of those self-service hand-wash places. I spent about ten bucks, which is double what the place costs for an automatic wash, but I wanted to give it a good scrub-down.

Funny thing is, when I went to the driver's door and studied the dent, it turned out it wasn't a dent at all. It was some kind of plastic residue. Like the little plastic-rubber strips they sometimes use to line the edges of car doors with.

Well, I guess that's all that hit my car.

It ended up coming right off in the wash.

ABOUT THE WRITERS

Christopher Beck is the author of numerous short stories and his work has appeared or is forthcoming in anthologies published by Dark Continents Publishing, May December Publications, Rainstorm Press, Inkbeans Press, and Black Hound.He lives in southern NJ where he continues to work on short and long fiction. Follow Chris at https://www.facebook.com/chrifive

Craig Caudill is a forty-two years old freelance writer. He studied Art History at Northern Kentucky University. Craig has been writing all his life with works in such literary journals as Falling Star Magazine, Front Magazine, Poetry Salzburg Review, and Neon Magazine. When not writing novels. Craig lives with his wife Gloria of ten years in Fort Mitchell Kentucky eating Sushi and Chicken Vindaloo.

Pete Clark has a number of short stories published on webzines, a story in Omnium Gatherum's 'Detritus' anthology and one in 'Short Sips' flash anthology for Wicked East Press, both published in 2012. He currently has three other upcoming print publications in 2012 for Wicked East Press. Recently awarded an Honorable Mention in the L. Ron Hubbard Writers of the Future contest, he includes Stephen King, Clive Barker and China Miéville among his many influences. Currently writing numerous short stories and the outline of a novel, he lives in North West England with his wife, two children and a growing collection of guitars.

Anthony Giangregorio is the author of 40 novels, almost all of them about zombies, and has edited over 40 anthologies and books. His work has appeared in Dead Science & Metahumans vs.

the Undead by Coscomentertainment, Dead Worlds: Undead Stories Volumes 1-7, and Wolves of War by Library of the Living Dead Press. He also has stories in End of Days: An Apocalyptic Anthology Vol. 1-5, the Book of the Dead series Vol. 1-6 by LDP, Zombie Zoology by Severed Press, and two anthologies with Pill Hill Press. He's also the creator of the 10 book action/zombie series titled Deadwater and the apocalyptic series Warriors of the Apocalypse. His action/horror novel Dead Rage is being optioned for a movie at this time.

Daniel Loubier is a relative up-and-comer in the horror genre. "Island Getaway" is the author's second publication under Open Casket Press. His zombie short, "A Family Tradition," was included in, "Dead Christmas: A Zombie Anthology" (Fall 2011). His work has also been featured on www.BrutalasHell.com, as part of their short fiction web series. His first novel, "Dead Summit," a zombie horror, was released in October. He's currently working on "Exorcising my Demon: The Biography of Eileen Dietz" (Fall 2012). To find out more about the author, visit him on Facebook (Daniel Loubier), Twitter (@DeadSummit), and on his website, www.danloubier.com

John Sabo lives on the South Side of Pittsburgh where he enjoys telling scary stories, watching slasher flicks, reading short horror stories and epic evil novels. He also enjoys preparing for the Zombie Apocalypse, surfing the web for spooky music, grilling 'all' kinds of meat and eating 'all' kinds of pizza. He's a work in progress that hasn't made very much progress thus far.

THE WAR AGAINST THEM: A ZOMBIE NOVEL
by Jose Alfredo Vazquez

Mankind wasn't prepared for the onslaught.

An ancient organism is reanimating the dead bodies of its victims, creating worldwide chaos and panic as the disease spreads to every corner of the globe. As governments struggle to contain the disease, courageous individuals across the planet learn what it truly means to make choices as they struggle to survive.

Geopolitics meet technology in a race to save mankind from the worst threat it has ever faced. Doctors, military and soldiers from all walks of life battle to find a cure. For the dead walk, and if not stopped, they will wipe out all life on Earth. Humanity is fighting a war they cannot win, for who can overcome Death itself? Man versus the walking dead with the winner ruling the planet. Welcome to *The War Against Them*.

THE TURNING: A STORY OF THE LIVING DEAD
by Kelly M. Hudson

The Dead Walk!

And no place on earth is safe from their ravening hunger. Civilization falls, leaving groups of struggling survivors to navigate a world that has descended into Hell.
Jeff Richards is one such survivor. He and his lover Jenny flee their home in the Bay Area and take a perilous journey through Northern California into Oregon, seeking shelter in rural areas to avoid both the living dead and that most treacherous animal of all: their fellow humans.
But can a man who has lost everything, including his humanity, ever be reborn? When the dead walk, will any of us survive?
Or will we all join the ranks of the undead to forever walk the earth.

END OF DAYS: AN APOCALYPTIC ANTHOLOGY
VOLUMES 1-5

Edited by Anthony Giangregorio

Our world is a fragile place.

Meteors, famine, floods, nuclear war, solar flares, and hundreds of other calamities can plunge our small blue planet into turmoil in an instant.

What would you do if tomorrow the sun went super nova or the world was swallowed by water, submerging the world into the cold darkness of the ocean? This anthology explores some of those scenarios and plunges you into total annihilation. But remember, it's only a book, and tomorrow will come as it always does.

Or will it?

KINGDOM OF THE DEAD
by Anthony Giangregorio
THE DEAD HAVE RISEN!

In the dead city of Pittsburgh, two small enclaves struggle to survive, eking out an existence of hand to mouth.

But instead of working together, both groups battle for the last remaining fuel and supplies of a city filled with the living dead.

Six months after the initial outbreak, a lone helicopter arrives bearing two more survivors and a newborn baby. One enclave welcomes them, while the other schemes to steal their helicopter and escape the decaying city.

With no police, fire, or social services existing, the two will battle for dominance in the steel city of the walking dead. But when the dust settles, the question is: will the remaining humans be the winners, or the losers?

When the dead walk, the line between Heaven and Hell is so twisted and bent there is no line at all.

RISE OF THE DEAD
by Anthony Giangregorio
DEATH IS ONLY THE BEGINNING!

In less than forty-eight hours, more than half the globe was infected.

In another forty-eight, the rest would be enveloped.

The reason?

A science experiment gone horribly wrong which enabled the dead to walk, their flesh rotting on their bones even as they seek human prey.

Jeremy was an ordinary nineteen year old slacker. He partied too much and had done poorly in high school. After a night of drinking and drugs, he awoke to find the world a very different place from the one he'd left the night before.

The dead were walking and feeding on the living, and as Jeremy stepped out into a world gone mad, the dead spotting him alone and unarmed in the middle of the street, he had to wonder if he would live long enough to see his twentieth birthday.

THE CHRONICLES OF JACK PRIMUS
BOOK ONE
by Michael D. Griffiths

Beneath the world of normalcy we all live in lies another world, one where supernatural beings exist. These creatures of the night hunt us; want to feed on our very souls, though only a few know of their existence.

One such man is Jack Primus, who accidentally pierces the veil between this world and the next. With no other choice if he wants to live, he finds himself on the run, hunted by beings called the Xemmoni, an ancient race that sees humans as nothing but cattle. They want his soul, to feed on his very essence, and they will kill all who stand in their way. But if they thought Jack would just lie down and accept his fate, they were sorely mistaken. He didn't ask for this battle, but he knew he would fight them with everything at his disposal, for to lose is a fate worse than death.

He would win this war, and he would take down anyone who got in his way.

ETERNAL NIGHT: A VAMPIRE ANTHOLOGY

Edited by Anthony Giangregorio

Blood, fangs, darkness and terror...these are the calling cards of the vampire mythos.

Inside this tome are stories that embrace vampire history but seek to introduce a new literary spin on this longstanding fictional monster Follow a dark journey through cigarette-smoking creatures hunted by rogue angels, vampires that feed off of thoughts instead of blood, immortals presenting the fantastic in a local rock band, to a legendary monster on the far reaches of town.

Forget what you know about vampires; this anthology will destroy historical mythos and embrace incredible new twists on this celebrated, fictional character.

Welcome to a world of the undead, welcome to the world of *Eternal Night*.

DEAD HISTORY 2

A Zombie Anthology

Edited by Anthony Giangregorio

From the dawn of mankind, the walking dead have been with us.

The greatest moments in history are not what they appear.

Through the ages, the undead have been there, only the proof has been erased, documents destroyed, and witnesses silenced.

The living dead is man's greatest secret.

In this tome, are a few of the stories of what really happened all those years ago. History isn't alive, it's dead!

INSIDE THE PERIMETER: SCAVENGERS OF THE DEAD

by Alan Spencer

In the middle of nowhere, the vestiges of an abandoned town are surrounded by inescapably high concrete barriers, permitting no trespass or escape. The town is dormant of human life, but rampant with the living dead, who choose not to eat flesh, but to instead continue their survival by cruder means.

Boyd Broman, a detective arrested and falsely imprisoned, has been transferred into the secret town. He is given an ultimatum: recapture Hayden Grubaugh, the cannibal serial killer, who has been banished to the town, in exchange for his freedom.

During Boyd's search, he discovers why the psychotic cannibal must really be captured and the sinister secrets the dead town holds.

With no chance of escape, Broman finds himself trapped among the ravenous, violent dead. With the cannibal feeding on the animated cadavers and the undead searching for Boyd, he must fulfill his end of the deal before the rotting corpses turn him into an unwilling organ donor.

But Boyd wasn't told that no one gets out alive, that the town is a death sentence. For there is no escape from *Inside the Perimeter*.

PLAYING GOD: A ZOMBIE NOVEL
by Jeffery Dye

It was supposed to be a regeneration virus to help soldiers on the battlefield— regrowing limbs and healing wounds— but a simple act of carelessness unleashed it on an unsuspecting world.

For the virus was not perfected, and once exposed, the host quickly dies, only to rise again as one of the undead.

As countries are quickly overrun, scientists and military teams battle to contain the outbreak.

There is no other option.

If the infection continues to spread, soon the entire globe will be consumed. And perhaps that will be a just punishment for a mankind that dared to try to play God.

DEAD HOUSE: A ZOMBIE GHOST STORY
by Keith Adam Luethke

The old mansion on the edge of town, aptly named Dead House, has a history of blood, pain, and death, but what Victor Leeds knows of this past only scratches the surface of the true horrors within.

But when his girlfriend is attacked by a shadowy figure one rainy night, he soon finds himself caught up in a world where the dead walk and ghostly wraiths abound. And to make matters worse, a pair of serial killers are fulfilling carefully made plans, and when they are done, the small town of Stormville, New York will run red. The last ingredient to open the gates of Hell, and plunge this small upstate town into madness, is rain.

And in Stormville, it pours by the gallons.

DROPPING FEAR
by Mike Catalano

On a dark night 25 years ago, masked maniac Derek Haddonfear went on a bloody rampage... Today, Derek's son, Will, is happily married, but still struggles to distance himself from the harsh memory of his father. He and his wife, Kerri, have been trying to get pregnant for years with zero success. Infertility begins to take its toll on their marriage.

Kerri can't live without becoming a mother and Will can't live seeing his wife so distraught. Upon coming into contact with a doctor working on an experimental fertility drug, a desperate Will and Kerri decide to give him a shot.

What results from the procedure sends Kerri on an uncontrollably violent path that is all too familiar to Will. Is it her hormones? Is it the drug? Or is Will's chilling past coming back to haunt him in the most bizarre of fashions? Regardless, no one will be prepared for the birth of the newest and most unexpected psychotic slasher in the history of horror.

ZOMBIES, MONSTERS, CREATURES OF THE NIGHT

OPEN CASKET PRESS

OPEN CASKET PRESS.COM

THE NEW NAME IN HORROR

UNDEAD PRESS

Where the Dead
Never Sleep

UNDEADPRESS.COM

CLAN OF THE BIGFOOT

ANTHONY GIANGREGORIO

My Little Sister's a
ZOMBIE!
jhb '10
Mike Catalano
Jason Bailey

VICTORY OF THE DEAD

ANTHONY GIANGREGORIO

www.ingramcontent.com/pod-product-compliance
Lightning Source LLC
Chambersburg PA
CBHW071004120726
47910CB00004B/1373